PUFFIN BOOKS

The Touchstone

Andrew Norriss was born in Scotland in 1947, went to university in Ireland and taught history in a sixth-form college in England for ten years before becoming a full-time writer. In the course of twenty years, he has written and co-written some hundred and fifty episodes of situation comedies and children's drama for television, and has written four books for children, including *Aquila*, which won the Whitbread Children's Book of the Year in 1997.

He lives very contentedly with his wife and two children in a village in Hampshire, where he acts in the local dramatic society (average age sixty-two), sings in the church choir (average age seventy-two) and for real excitement travels to the cinema in Basingstoke.

Books by Andrew Norriss

AQUILA
BERNARD'S WATCH
MATT'S MILLION
THE TOUCHSTONE

ANDREW NORRISS

THE TOUCHSTONE

PUFFIN

PUFFIN BOOKS

Published by the Penguin Group
Penguin Books Ltd, 80 Strand, London WC2R 0RL, England
Penguin Putnam Inc., 375 Hudson Street, New York, New York 10014, USA
Penguin Books Australia Ltd, 250 Camberwell Road, Camberwell, Victoria 3124, Australia
Penguin Books Canada Ltd, 10 Alcorn Avenue, Toronto, Ontario, Canada M4V 3B2
Penguin Books India (P) Ltd, 11 Community Centre, Panchsheel Park, New Delhi – 110 017, India
Penguin Books (NZ) Ltd, Cnr Rosedale and Airborne Roads, Albany, Auckland, New Zealand
Penguin Books (South Africa) (Pty) Ltd, 24 Sturdee Avenue, Rosebank 2196, South Africa

Penguin Books Ltd, Registered Offices: 80 Strand, London WC2R 0RL, England

www.penguin.com

First published 2004
1

Set in Monotype Plantin
Typeset by Rowland Phototypesetting Ltd, Bury St Edmunds, Suffolk
Made and printed in England by Clays Ltd, St Ives plc

British Library Cataloguing in Publication Data
A CIP catalogue record for this book is available from the British Library

ISBN 0–141–30343–3

CHAPTER ONE

One morning, as Douglas was leaving for school, he heard a voice calling his name. It was a faint voice, hardly louder than the wind blowing through the trees, but when he looked round to see who was calling, there was nobody there.

He was wondering if he might have imagined it when the voice called again.

'Douglas!' it said, slightly louder this time but still hardly more than a whisper. Puzzled, he looked around him, but the garden in front of the house seemed quite deserted. Only when the voice called a third time, did he realize it was coming from one of the lilac bushes that ran along the wall in front of the road.

Crossing the grass, he pulled aside one of the branches and found a woman sitting on the ground with her back against the wall, her chin on her chest and her right hand clutching her left shoulder. She was wearing black boots, combat trousers and a khaki sleeveless vest.

Resting in her lap was a case made of a dull grey metal, about as big as the lunchbox Douglas had used when he was in primary school. Around her neck, hanging on a silver chain, was a green stone, the size of the top joint of a man's thumb.

As Douglas pulled aside the branch to look at her, she lifted her head.

'Douglas?' It was the voice that had been calling him and he could understand now why it had been so faint. Speaking seemed to take a considerable effort. 'Douglas Paterson?'

Douglas wondered how the woman knew his name. He had never seen her before in his life. Pushing the branch he was holding to one side, he knelt beside her.

'Are you all right?'

'I am hurt,' said the woman in a hoarse whisper.

'I'll get someone to help.' Douglas stood up. There was no one in the house as his mother had already left for work, but he could phone the emergency services and ask for an ambulance.

'No!' The hand that reached out and grasped his arm was surprisingly strong. 'No one must know I am here. If they find me, I am lost.'

'Oh,' said Douglas. 'Right . . .'

'I do not have much time, so you must listen carefully. Three things.' She spoke in short bursts, breathing through clenched teeth between each of them. 'One, my name is Kai and I come from another planet. Two, my mission is to take this . . .' she gestured to the case in her lap, '. . . back to my home world and liberate my people. Three, I am being hunted by the Guardians of the Federation and my only chance of escape is to find someone to hide me for the next forty-eight hours.' She looked up at Douglas, her dark eyes staring intently into his. 'Gedrus says you are the only *coda* I can reach. Will you help me? Please?'

Douglas did not reply immediately. For some seconds he knelt there, not moving or speaking.

'Please!' Kai tugged at his arm 'Will you help?'

With a start, Douglas shook himself out of his trance.

'Sorry,' he said. 'What was number one again?'

Douglas was not the sort of boy to panic when something out of the ordinary happened. In the battlefield of life, when shells and mortar bombs were falling all around, he was the one you would find in the corner of a dugout quietly making himself a cheese sandwich and brewing a pot of tea. If you wanted calm in the face of a crisis Douglas Paterson was your man, but even he found the next half-hour something of a strain.

The first of several shocks, as he unlocked the front door and helped Kai up the steps and into the house, was the way her left arm fell off. He picked it up, at her request, and pushed the end of it back into her shoulder socket – but it fell off again as they crossed the hall, and again as they struggled up the stairs.

In the end Douglas carried it himself until they got to his bedroom where Kai, gasping for breath, sat down on the bed and asked if he had anything that might hold it in place. Douglas went and got a roll of Elastoplast and a pair of scissors from the first-aid box in the bathroom.

He came back to the bedroom where Kai was still sitting on the bed, her left arm lying across the metal case on her lap and a blue gunge oozing slowly from her shoulder socket. In her right hand she was holding the green crystal that hung from the chain around her neck. Her eyes were half-closed and her lips moved slightly, as if she was talking to someone. Douglas wondered if she was saying a prayer.

When she looked up, she nodded approvingly at the tape and scissors.

'Excellent.' Letting go of the crystal, she picked up her left arm and held it in place. 'Two strips will be sufficient. They will be needed for only a few hours.'

Douglas unrolled a strip of tape, cut it off and ran it round the top of Kai's arm and on to her body. As he reached for a second piece, he was about to mention that he still thought calling an ambulance might be a good idea, when Kai started talking again.

'I will tell you what is going to happen, Douglas. In

a few minutes I will become unconscious. I will be like that for two days. For forty-eight hours, you understand? During that time my body will heal. It is very important that I am left alone while this is happening.' She looked directly at him to emphasize what she was saying. 'I will not need food or water. I will not need help or medical care. I will need, only, to be left alone.' She looked around the room. 'You can put me where you like. The only thing that is important is that my hiding place remain a secret.'

She reached up to take Douglas's hand as he stuck the second piece of tape over her shoulder.

'I must not be found. And you must tell no one of my presence here. Gedrus says that if you speak to anyone, anyone at all, I will almost certainly be caught.'

Douglas opened his mouth to speak but Kai lifted her hand to silence him.

'I know. You have many questions, but I do not have the time to answer them. However, I have something that may reassure you.'

Releasing Douglas, Kai touched the front of the metal case on her lap with the fingers of her right hand and the lid swung open. Inside, laid out in a row, were three green stones, identical to the one Kai wore around her neck. In fact, the way the stones were spaced made Douglas think that the stone she wore had once been the fourth.

Each of the stones was attached to a silver chain

and they lay in the case as if buried in glass, like one of those paperweights where a flower or an insect is held inside a glass ball.

'Take one.' Kai pointed to the case and then, when Douglas hesitated. 'Here . . .'

She took his hand and pushed it into the case. Douglas found that what had looked like solid glass felt and moved like a liquid. It offered no more resistance than a bowl of water as he grasped one of the silver chains and pulled it free. The solid surface reformed beneath his hand with barely a ripple. He stared at it, and then at the stone that hung from the chain on his fingers.

'It is called a Touchstone,' said Kai. 'You hold it like this.' She clenched her hand around the crystal that hung round her own neck.

Slowly Douglas reached up and curled his fingers round the stone. He instantly felt a shock wave of energy that seemed to travel in a split second from the stone in his hand to every nerve-ending in his body. Up his arm to the hairs on his head and down to the end of his toes, a wave of vital, tingling awareness shot through him and, with a cry of surprise, he opened his fingers and dropped the crystal as if he had been burnt.

Kai looked at him, her dark eyes staring out from a face that was growing paler by the second.

'From now on, when there is anything you don't understand, anything you need to know, any time you need help, you hold the stone and you ask Gedrus. You understand?'

'Gedrus?'

'He can tell you whatever you need to know.'

Carefully closing the lid of the case, she put a hand on Douglas's shoulder and pulled herself up. Standing, she looked directly into his face.

'But it is important that you let no one see it. No one must know that you have it. No one . . .' Kai's face was completely drained of colour now and she began to sway. 'The time is very close. We must choose now where you would like to conceal me because soon . . . soon, I shall . . .'

Her eyes closed and Kai toppled sideways to the floor, her body landing on the boards with a crash that seemed to echo round the house.

Douglas stared at her for several seconds before kneeling down beside her to hold her wrist. There was no sign of a pulse but, since he was holding the arm that had fallen off, that was not entirely surprising. Nor was there any sign of breathing. In fact, no indication that Kai was alive at all.

Douglas wondered what he should do and eventually decided that he would have to phone for help. He was twelve years old and he knew that twelve-year-old boys do not hide dead bodies in their bedrooms for two days, even if that is what the dead person wants and they have promised to get better.

He shifted his position to stand up and, as he did so,

brushed his knee against the green stone, which was lying on the floor where he had dropped it. Almost without thinking, he picked it up and the result was as instantaneous as it was dramatic.

This time there was no shock but directly in front of his face a picture appeared, hanging in space like a window in the air. It was about a metre square and astonishingly vivid. Each part of it was crystal clear, the colours wonderfully bright, the detail pinpoint sharp – and the image it presented was every bit as real as the room around him.

The picture was of a library. An enormous room, where hundreds of shelves containing thousands of books stretched in all directions as far as the eye could see. At the front, a young man was sitting in a swivel chair with his feet propped up on a large desk, reading a book and eating an apple.

As Douglas stared, the man looked up from his book and gave a little nod of recognition, as if he and Douglas were old acquaintances passing the time of day in the street.

'Hi there!' he smiled cheerfully. 'What can I do for you?'

There was a long pause.

'Who are you?' asked Douglas.

The man in the picture leaned forward and pointed to the word written in gold letters on a triangular piece of wood on the front of his desk.

'I,' he said, 'am Gedrus.'

CHAPTER TWO

'You might like to think of me,' Gedrus leant forward with his elbows on the desk, 'as the sort of access point to an encyclopaedia.' He gestured to the rows of books behind him. 'A very large encyclopaedia that contains information about events and people from all corners of the galaxy. Anything you want to know, you hold the stone, ask me, and I will give you the answer.'

'Anything?' asked Douglas.

'Pretty much.' Gedrus shrugged modestly. 'As encyclopaedias go, I'm kind of big.'

Douglas pointed to the figure on the floor. 'Do you know who this is?'

'That is the body of Kai Akka Kahkousi.' The name, as Gedrus pronounced it, sounded like a baby coughing. 'She is a native of the planet Vangar, which orbits a star in the constellation of Taurus.'

Douglas stared at the body on the floor, then at Gedrus, and then back at the body. 'She really is from another planet?'

'Yes.'

'Is she dead?'

'Her body has shut down for regeneration,' said Gedrus. 'It's a process that will take about forty-eight hours. After that she'll be fine.'

'I don't have to do anything to help? I just have to leave her alone?'

'No outside assistance is required,' said Gedrus happily. 'Only time.'

There was a long pause while Douglas continued to stare at the body.

'Was there anything else you wanted to ask?'

'Yes.' Douglas walked towards the window, the picture of Gedrus moving in front of him as he went. 'She told me she had to get that,' he pointed to the grey metal case Kai still held in her right hand, 'to her home planet. To liberate her people.'

'Yes?'

'And she said she was being chased by the Guardians of the Federation who wanted to stop her.'

'Yes?'

'Well,' Douglas hesitated. 'Was that all true as well?'

'It certainly was,' Gedrus nodded, his face becoming serious. 'They hunt her, even as we speak, with everything they have.'

'So she wasn't lying or anything?'

'Everything she told you was the truth,' said Gedrus. It looked for a moment as if he was going to say something else but instead he reached for a banana from the fruit bowl on his desk.

Douglas looked around the room. If he was going to hide Kai's body, as she had asked, there were a limited number of places he could put it. She was a tall, well-built woman and he doubted if he could carry her very far. He put down the Touchstone on his desk under the window and the picture of Gedrus and the library disappeared as he walked back to the body on the floor.

When Kai fell, all but her head had landed on a rug that ran along the side of his bed. Under the rug, the floor was of polished wood and he found that, with some effort, he was able to slide both the body and the carpet under the bed. When he had pushed them as far as he could he placed the metal case with the remaining Touchstones beside Kai's head, then pulled down the duvet so that it hung over the side of the bed, hiding everything from view.

He came back to the window and picked up the Touchstone the alien had given him.

'Hi there!' Gedrus looked up from his book again. 'What can I do for you?'

'I just thought I'd tell you that I'm off now,' said Douglas. 'I have to go to school.'

'Have a nice day!' said Gedrus.

*

At school Douglas usually ate lunch with his friends at a table in the dining room, but he decided today that he would rather be alone. He needed time to think, so he took his sandwiches to a bench behind the science block that looked out over the playing field.

He was not alone for very long, however. After a few minutes he was joined by Ivo Radomir, a boy in the same class as Douglas, though not someone he knew well. He was from Bulgaria and had joined the school in the middle of the previous term.

'I saw your name in the late book this morning.' Ivo reached into his bag and took out what looked like a large jar of yoghurt. 'Did you get into trouble?'

The school's headmaster, Mr Linneker, had a reputation for being particularly fierce with people who were late. In a recent assembly he had threatened to put the letter L with a branding iron on the forehead of anyone who was late, though Ivo had found out afterwards that this was probably a joke.

'No,' said Douglas. 'Not really.'

Ivo was not entirely surprised. He had noticed before that teachers did not treat Douglas the way they treated most pupils. They did not shout at him or get angry, though this may have been because Douglas rarely did the sort of things that made teachers want to shout or get angry in the first place.

'I was late. I got a detention.' Ivo put down his yoghurt for a moment and took out a fist-sized metal object from his bag. 'But it was worth it. I was getting this from a skip. It's the electric motor from a washing machine.' He passed it over for Douglas to inspect. 'I'm going to use it in the robot I'm building.'

'A robot,' said Douglas politely. 'How interesting.'

People did not usually express an interest when Ivo started talking about his robot, and he was glad of the chance to explain exactly how he was planning to build it in the shed at the bottom of his garden.

'You could come and help if you like,' he said as he took out a set of plans and spread them out over Douglas's lunchbox. 'After school perhaps. Today if you want.'

'That's very kind of you,' said Douglas, 'but I can't today. There's a . . . a problem I have to deal with at home.'

He left soon after that and Ivo, watching him go, wondered what the problem could be. He had always imagined that Douglas was the sort of person who never had any problems at all.

Douglas got home from school at four o'clock, let himself into the house and went straight upstairs to his bedroom to see what, if anything, had happened to Kai.

The body was still where he had put it, under the bed, but it did not look quite as he had left it that morning. The skin had turned grey and patches of it, particularly on Kai's face and arms, had begun to peel away. In sections it had opened up, and more of the blue sticky stuff he had seen when Kai's arm fell off was bubbling up in blisters, to sit on the surface in scabby lumps.

She looked very dead.

Douglas went over to the cupboard where he kept his clothes and took the Touchstone from its hiding place under a pile of socks. As his fingers curled round the crystal, the picture of Gedrus in the library appeared in front of him, sitting at his desk, making a plastic model of a Lancaster bomber.

'Hi there!' He looked up. 'What can I do for you?'

'Is she all right?' Douglas pointed to the body under the bed. 'Only she's gone a funny colour. Sort of grey.'

'Perfectly normal.' Gedrus carefully glued a propeller in place. 'Nothing to worry about. All going the way it's supposed to.'

'Good.'

There was a pause.

'Anything else you wanted to ask?'

'Yes.' There was something that had been bothering Douglas most of the day, though he wasn't sure if it was the sort of question Gedrus would be able to answer.

'Why me?' he asked.

'I'm sorry?'

'Why would an alien who wants help come to me? There's millions of people around, why not ask somebody . . . older?'

'Ah,' Gedrus smiled, 'well, it was my suggestion really.'

'Yours?'

Gedrus nodded. 'Not that there was much choice, to be honest. She was hurt, you see. The life-pod was breaking up. By the time she reached the ground we knew she couldn't walk far and you were the only *coda* she could reach.'

Douglas remembered that Kai had used the same phrase. 'What's a coder?'

'A *coda*,' Gedrus flicked a switch on his desk and the word appeared on a screen behind him in large letters, 'is a term from the Tenebrian Personality Profiling System. It describes your chief personality characteristics. The C means that you are the sort of person who can absorb new and disturbing information without too much emotion – in other words you don't panic. The O means you're someone who likes his privacy, so you're the sort of person who can keep a secret. The D means you're completely honest and dependable, and the A means you have a very trusting personality and tend to believe what someone tells you as long as it doesn't contradict common sense or something you already know.' Gedrus leaned back in his chair. 'It's an unusual combination of characteristics. In fact, you're the only category 1 *coda* in the county.'

There was a long pause as Douglas absorbed this information.

'Anything else you'd like to ask about?' said Gedrus.

Douglas looked at his watch. He had about an hour before his mother got home from work.

'Yes,' he said, firmly. 'Quite a lot really.'

Mrs Paterson had recently started working on a check-out desk at the local supermarket. It was not a job she enjoyed and she was always glad to get home.

Normally she would cook supper in the kitchen while Douglas did his homework. They would talk about what they had done in their day and after they had eaten they would go through to the sitting room and watch television together. But that evening she hardly saw Douglas at all. He stayed in his room until supper was ready and when he had eaten, went straight back up again.

Mrs Paterson went up at about eight o'clock to ask if he was all right, and heard him talking. He was speaking very quietly and from outside on the landing she could not hear what he was saying. When she pushed open the door, she found him sitting at his desk staring straight at her, but for several seconds he didn't seem to see her or give any sign that he knew she was there. When she asked what the talking had been about, all he would say was that he had been working something out in his head

The counsellor had warned her that, though Douglas had taken the news of the divorce very calmly, she could expect some odd and even disruptive behaviour as time went on. Perhaps this was what he had meant.

Mrs Paterson did not like the idea. It was bad enough to have messed up her own life without thinking she had messed up her son's as well.

CHAPTER THREE

Douglas's mother noticed the smell as soon as she opened the door to his bedroom the next morning. It was a seriously bad smell. Like drains, or possibly a dead animal somewhere under the floorboards.

Mrs Paterson was a woman who liked the things around her to be clean and tidy. She found bad smells upsetting and what upset her even more was the knowledge that, in the old days, Archie would have been there to sort it out for her. Archie was the one who knew about checking drains and pulling up floorboards to look for dead mice, but Archie had gone. Mr Paterson was no longer there to sort out this or a hundred other things.

For an awful moment Douglas thought his mother was going to insist on clearing everything out of his room and finding the source of the smell then and there, but she decided in the end that there wasn't time. The manager of the supermarket where she worked was almost as fussy about people being late as Mr Linneker, and she told Douglas the problem would have to wait until she got back in the evening.

Douglas had realized where the smell was coming from as soon as he woke up and, after his mother had left, he lifted the duvet and looked under his bed to see what had happened.

Kai's body had undergone more changes during the night. Her arms and face were now covered in crusty blue scabs the size of biscuits. On her chest and shoulders whole sections of her skin were peeling off. Clumps of her hair had fallen out, and there were holes all over her clothes, as if they had been burnt by a giant cigarette end.

Douglas took out the Touchstone from the drawer of his bedside table and found Gedrus at his desk in the library, eating a bowl of cornflakes.

'Hi there!' He gave Douglas a wave. 'What can I do for you?'

'It's Kai's body,' said Douglas. 'It smells really bad and it looks awful.'

'All part of the regeneration process.' Gedrus smiled reassuringly. 'As the old organs decompose, you see, and the new ones are manufactured, the body needs to get rid of various wastes, so it pushes some of them out in the form of corrosive acids and noxious gases.'

'Corrosive acids?'

'That's why bits of her clothes and shoes are rotting away.'

Douglas could not help feeling that it might have been useful to have been warned about this the day before, but there didn't seem any point in saying so.

'The thing is,' he said, 'when my mother gets back from work, she's going to come up here to look for what's causing the smell and she's going to find the body, isn't she?'

'Not much chance of her missing it,' Gedrus agreed.

'So what do I do?'

'About what?'

'About the body,' said Douglas. 'How do I make sure nobody finds it for the next twenty-four hours?'

'Ah.' Gedrus did not hesitate. 'If you want to keep it hidden, I'd suggest moving it to the bathroom in the annexe.'

Douglas's house was a large one. As well as the five bedrooms, two bathrooms and three reception rooms in the main house, there was a self-contained flat attached to the side. It was called a granny flat but since Douglas's grandparents lived very happily in their own homes, at the moment it was only used for storing spare furniture.

It would be, Douglas realized, the perfect hiding place. Nobody went there, so nobody would complain about the smell and, when Kai recovered, he could wash away any corrosive acids and bits of skin and hair she might leave behind, by turning on the taps and flushing them down the drain.

There was still one problem, however.

'She's very heavy.' Douglas remembered that simply pushing Kai's body under the bed the day before had been an effort. He doubted if he would be able to carry it down the stairs to the annexe and lift it into the bath. 'How do I get her there?'

'Well, I don't think you'd manage it on your own.' Gedrus tapped thoughtfully on the desk with the end of his spoon. 'You'll need someone to help.'

'But I can't get anyone to help, can I? Kai said I wasn't to tell anyone. She said if I did she'd be caught and put in prison. You said the same thing yourself.'

'I believe,' Gedrus turned to consult a large desk diary, 'that we both said being caught would be *almost* a certainty if you told anyone. But a lot depends on who you tell. There is one person you could ask to help, who could be trusted to keep the secret.'

'Who?' asked Douglas.

And the answer was quite a surprise.

Ivo Radomir was not the sort of boy who made friends easily. This was partly because he was Bulgarian, had ears that stuck out from the side of his head and a seriously bad haircut, but also because he had always found it easier to connect with machines than with other people. They were easier to understand,

and they didn't walk away while you were talking to them.

Ivo usually had lunch on his own, on the bench behind the science lab, and that was where Douglas came to find him. He was making himself a sandwich, cutting a piece of bread from a loaf with his pocket knife and then slicing an onion to put on top. He generously offered to share it with Douglas.

Douglas shook his head. 'No thanks,' he said. 'I came down here to ask for your help. But before I tell you what it's about, you have to promise to keep it a secret. You mustn't tell anyone else about it. Ever.'

Ivo was rather flattered. People did not often ask for his help or to share secrets with him but, as Douglas went on to tell him about finding an alien in the garden, the Touchstone, and needing help to move a dead body to a downstairs bathroom, he became increasingly alarmed. He wondered if, like the headmaster's branding iron, this was some English idea of a joke, but Douglas insisted that he was serious. He said he knew what Ivo must be thinking and there was a very simple way to prove he was telling the truth.

'This is the stone she gave me.' From his pocket Douglas took out a handkerchief and unwrapped it to reveal the Touchstone. 'It can give you a bit of a shock the first time you hold it, but when you see the man in the library he'll be able to tell you it's all true.'

Ivo reached out and took the stone. Holding it in his fingers, he peered out over the playing fields but, however hard he looked, there was no picture in the air, no library and no Gedrus.

Douglas wondered, briefly, if Ivo had somehow broken it but when he took back the stone, the image of Gedrus appeared immediately. The librarian had his feet up on the desk, and was reading a copy of the *Beano*.

'Hi there!' He smiled as cheerfully as ever. 'What can I do for you?'

Douglas turned to Ivo. 'Can you see him now?'

'See who?' Ivo looked blankly in the direction Douglas was pointing. All he could see was grass and the football posts.

Douglas turned back to Gedrus. 'Why can't he see you?'

'That would be because I'm not an external physical reality,' Gedrus explained. 'I'm an image produced in your brain. It's only the person holding the stone who can see me.'

'But when Ivo had the stone, he couldn't see you then either.'

'No.' Gedrus nodded sympathetically.

'Why not?'

'Touchstones are designed to be used by only one person,' said Gedrus. 'The first person to touch it is the only one who can ever use it. It's a security thing. Means there's no point stealing someone else's.'

Douglas turned to Ivo. 'He says I'm the only one who can see him because he's only a picture made in

23

my brain.' He thought rapidly. 'But we can still prove I'm not making it up. All you have to do is ask him a question.'

'A question?'

'He knows everything, so he can answer anything you ask.'

Ivo paused, a slice of bread and onion halfway to his mouth, and thought for a moment.

'What's the capital of Sweden?'

'It's Stockholm,' said Douglas. 'But I already knew that. You have to ask him something I wouldn't know the answer to, but you do.'

'Oh.' Ivo thought again. 'All right. What's the name of the village in Bulgaria where my mother was born?'

Douglas looked at Gedrus.

'Do you know what village . . .'

'I'm ahead of you on this one, Douglas.' Gedrus was looking up the answer in a large leather-bound book he had pulled from one of the shelves. 'And the answer is Klisura in the Valley of the Roses.'

'He says it was Klisura,' said Douglas. 'In the Valley of the Roses.'

Ivo blinked. 'And my father?'

'That was in Hisarya,' said Gedrus.

'That was in Hisarya,' said Douglas.

Ivo slowly put down his sandwich. 'How could you know that?'

'I didn't.' Douglas placed the stone back on the

24

handkerchief. 'Gedrus told me. I told you. He knows everything.'

'Everything?'

Douglas gave a little shrug. 'He's been able to answer anything I've asked.' He paused. 'Well? Will you help?'

'What?' Ivo was still staring at the Touchstone in Douglas's lap.

'Moving this body. After school.'

'Oh, yes,' said Ivo, slowly. 'Sure.' He pointed to the Touchstone and added, thoughtfully, 'You haven't got a sparc one of those, have you?'

When school ended Douglas took Ivo back to his house, led him upstairs to his bedroom and pulled Kai's body out from under the bed.

The alien looked, if anything, even worse than she had that morning. The scabs on her face and chest were larger and crustier than ever, her hair had disappeared altogether and whole sections of her clothing and skin were hanging off her body like loose wallpaper.

Ivo stared at the body in undisguised horror. 'She's dead!' he said.

'I know it looks that way but . . .'

'No! She doesn't just *look* that way,' said Ivo, 'she is! She's dead!'

'Only technically.' Douglas knelt beside the body and pulled on a pair of rubber gloves he had got from the kitchen. 'You see this?' He pointed to Kai's left shoulder. 'This is the arm that fell off yesterday. I had to put tape on to hold it in place, but look at it now.' He tapped the blue scab that had formed around the join. 'The tape's fallen off but the arm's still there, and all this stuff seems to be holding it in place. And look at this.' He picked up Kai's arm, bent it, and let it fall again. 'Dead bodies go stiff and she's not doing that at all. She's regenerating.' He stood up. 'Gedrus is very definite. All we have to do is put her somewhere safe and by tomorrow morning she'll be fine.'

Looking at the body on the floor, Ivo fought back the urge to run screaming back out to the street. He wanted to help if he could.

The truth was that Douglas was one of the few people who ever spoke to Ivo at school. He said hello in the morning, had lent Ivo his pencil on more than one occasion, and rescued his bag once when some other boys had thought it would be fun to throw it round the classroom. It might not sound much, but if you're a Bulgarian with ears that stick out at an English comprehensive, you remember when people are nice to you, if only because it doesn't happen that often.

Ivo had been brought up with a strong sense of duty. Douglas had been kind to him at times when it would have been very easy not to bother, and now it was time for that kindness to be returned.

'OK,' he said. 'What do I have to do?'

'Put these on.' Douglas passed him a pair of rubber gloves. 'They'll stop the acid getting on your hands. Then you can take her legs.'

With Ivo at one end of the body and Douglas at the other, they wrapped Kai in the rug, dragged her out on to the landing and hauled her down the stairs. At the bottom Ivo waited while Douglas got the key to the annexe from its hook on the back of the pantry door. Then they dragged the rug across the floor of the annexe hall and into the bathroom.

Even with two of them, lifting up the body and tipping it into the bath wasn't easy, but they finally managed it. Later, Douglas thought, he would have to ask Gedrus what to do about the rug, but for now he left it on the floor under the washbasin and put the metal case with the other Touchstones on top of it. The two boys stood there a moment, catching their breath and staring down at the figure in the bath.

'She's supposed to wake up about nine o'clock tomorrow morning,' Douglas said eventually. 'I was hoping you could be around then as well, you know, in case she needed any help.'

Ivo wondered briefly what sort of help a dead person might need when they woke up, and then he wondered what Mr Linneker would do if he was late for school twice in one week.

'What's going to happen exactly?' he asked. 'When she wakes up?'

'I've no idea,' said Douglas. 'I suppose we'll find out tomorrow.'

Mrs Paterson was relieved to find when she got home that the smell in Douglas's bedroom had disappeared. She still put his clothes and bedding through the washing machine to be on the safe side, but fortunately it was one problem that seemed to have resolved itself.

If she no longer had to worry about the smell, however, she was still worried about Douglas. This was the second day that he had spent the whole evening up in his room. Twice she had gone up to ask if he would like to join her in the sitting room, but both times he had said he was busy – which was obviously untrue. Each time she went up he had been sitting on his bed, not reading, not working, not doing anything – just sitting there, staring into space.

It was very worrying, and Mrs Paterson did what she always did when she was worried. She rolled back the carpet in the drawing room, put a CD in the music centre, closed her eyes . . . and danced.

Before she married, Mrs Paterson had done a lot of ballroom dancing – she had been Home Counties Latin American champion three years in a row – but all that had stopped when she met Archie. Archie was not interested in dancing and soon after they were married Douglas was born, and Mrs Paterson found herself quite busy enough looking after her home, her husband and her son.

But she still found that nothing helped take her mind off a problem more effectively than the familiar rhythmic patterns of a dance. Latin American was best, especially if she was worrying about something. A samba perhaps, or a *paso doble*. Or if she was *really* worried, the rumba.

Tonight, she decided, was definitely a time for the rumba.

CHAPTER FOUR

The next morning, after his mother had left for work, Douglas collected the annexe key from its place on the back of the pantry door and was crossing the hall to the annexe entrance when Ivo rang the front door bell. He had been waiting outside until he had seen Mrs Paterson leave, then scurried up the drive to the door.

'Has anything happened?' he asked as Douglas let him in. 'Is she still dead?'

'I don't know,' said Douglas. 'I haven't looked yet.'

Together the boys walked down the corridor of the annexe to the bathroom where they found Kai lying in the bath, but looking very different from the peeling, scab-ridden corpse they had placed there the day before.

'Wow . . .' breathed Ivo.

And Douglas could only agree. The old skin had completely sloughed away from Kai's body, and the new skin beneath was clear and pink. All the crusted blue scabs had fallen away, there was no trace of a scar where her left arm joined to the shoulder and the hair that had grown back on her head was already several inches long.

The changes were all clearly visible because most of Kai's clothes had fallen away along with her old skin. A few shreds of cloth still hung here and there, but mostly they had been eaten away by the acids her body had produced. Only the Touchstone had been unaffected. It lay on her chest, glittering quietly in the light from the window.

Douglas had brought a dressing gown from his mother's bedroom and he draped it carefully over the body before sitting down beside Ivo on the laundry basket to wait. Gedrus had said that Kai would revive a little before nine o'clock and there were still twenty minutes to go.

At five past nine they were still waiting and Douglas was about to ask Gedrus if anything had gone wrong when Kai's body suddenly flung back its head, drew in a huge, rasping breath and sat bolt upright in the bath. A moment later the breaths were coming thick and fast, as if Kai were a drowning woman desperate for oxygen, and then her breathing slowed, her eyes opened and she turned to face the boys.

'Hi,' said Douglas. 'How are you feeling?'

Kai did not answer at once. Instead, her hand curled round the Touchstone hanging from her neck as she looked, not at Douglas but at Ivo, sitting beside him. Her lips moved as if she was talking to herself and Douglas guessed she was asking Gedrus a question. Whatever she asked – and the boys could hear neither the question nor the reply – she seemed satisfied with the answer she got.

'You are Ivo,' she said. It was a statement, not a question, and Ivo nodded nervously in reply.

'I had to tell him about you,' said Douglas. 'I know you said not to tell anyone but if I hadn't . . .'

Kai held up a hand. 'You have the case?'

Douglas picked up the grey metal case from under the washbasin and gave it to Kai. She took it and opened it. There were still two Touchstones inside.

'They're still there,' said Douglas. 'We didn't take them.'

'It is well.' Kai leaned back in the bath. 'It is very well.'

There was a pause while she lay there for a moment with her eyes closed and then she spoke again. 'I will need food. Food and water.'

'I could probably find you something in the kitchen,' said Douglas. 'If you'd like to come through?'

Kai stood up, letting fall a shower of skin flakes, scraps of clothing and the dressing gown as she did so. She stepped out of the bath and prepared to follow the boys through to the main house.

32

It was Douglas who suggested that it might be a good idea to put on the dressing gown first.

She ate an astonishing amount of food, mostly bread and baked beans, and drank nearly eight pints of water. Douglas and Ivo watched from the other end of the kitchen table as she pushed the last corner of toast into her mouth and sat back with a gentle belch.

'I thank you.' It was the first time she had spoken since sitting down. 'I thank you both for all you have done for me.'

'What happens now?' asked Douglas.

'Now I will return to my world and fulfil the rest of my mission.'

'But I thought you didn't have a ship any more?'

Kai shrugged. 'I shall build another.'

'How?'

'I have Gedrus.' Kai fingered the stone around her neck. 'He will show me how. As he will show me how to liberate my people.'

'He can do that?'

'He can.' Kai smiled. 'That is the reason I stole this.' She pointed to the metal case on the table beside her.

'You stole it?' For some reason Douglas had always presumed that the stones belonged to Kai and that the Guardians were trying to steal them from her.

'I had no choice.' Kai pushed back her chair and stood up. 'The Guardians believe that only they have the right to hold a Touchstone. But if my people are to be free, Gedrus is their only chance. He can tell us what weapons we need and how to build them. He can tell us what we have to do and how to prepare. He can tell us what the tyrant is planning and how we can defeat him. Without Gedrus we could not win, but with him we cannot lose.'

There was a fierce, cold look to Kai's face as she spoke that almost made Douglas feel sorry for the tyrant, or anyone else who stood in her way, but when she looked across at Douglas her face softened. 'Before I leave, may I presume upon your hospitality one last time?'

'What is it?'

'I will need clothes.' The dressing gown Kai was wearing was several sizes too small for her and definitely not something to be worn out of doors. 'Is there something I could borrow?'

Douglas had a feeling that any of his mother's clothes would not only be too small but somehow . . . not right. As Ivo said later, you could dress Kai in a leather jerkin and give her a battleaxe to hold and she would have looked quite presentable, but in one of Mrs Paterson's dresses she would just look weird.

'Gedrus tells me,' Kai was fingering the Touchstone again, 'that in a wardrobe in the spare back bedroom are a pair of jeans and a flannel shirt which . . .'

She stopped suddenly, tilting her head to one side

34

as if listening, and a moment later Douglas heard the sound of a key turning in the front door.

Although Mr Paterson no longer lived with his wife and son, he still had a key to the house in Western Avenue. He was using it now to collect some boxes of books and a few other personal possessions to take back to his flat. It was something he preferred to do when he knew Mrs Paterson was not at home. It saved them both a lot of awkwardness.

As he let himself into the house he heard a noise and, walking through to the kitchen, was surprised to find Douglas and one of his school friends putting dishes into the sink.

'Douglas?' It was half past nine and his son was supposed to be at school. 'What's going on?'

'This is Ivo,' said Douglas. 'He's in my class.'

'Hello, Ivo.' Mr Paterson frowned as he looked around the kitchen. 'And who's the other visitor?'

'Other visitor?'

'Three glasses on the table, the utility room door closes as I come in, wet footprints . . .' Mr Paterson pointed to the floor by the chair where Kai had been sitting. 'I can see someone else is here. Who is it?'

There was an embarrassing silence while the boys tried to think of a reply and then there was the sound of a lavatory flushing, the door to the utility room opened and Kai appeared.

She was dressed as a schoolgirl – if you could

imagine Sheena the Warrior Princess in school uniform. She was wearing a short black skirt, a white shirt, a school tie, and the hair at the side of her head had been pulled into bunches with a couple of elastic bands. Though the shirt was clearly too small for her, she had tied the ends in a knot under her chest, leaving a bare midriff, in a way that was rather stylish.

She came straight over to Mr Paterson. 'You must be Douglas's father.' She held out a hand. 'How nice to meet you. I am Kay.'

'Archie Paterson.' Douglas's father looked slightly bemused as he shook hands.

'I hope you don't mind my being here,' Kai went on, 'but the boys have been helping me with some work.'

'Really?'

'They have been showing me how to set out the graphics for my sociology project.' Kai's eyelashes fluttered as she spoke. 'I am not very good at computers myself.'

'Oh, I see!' Mr Paterson nodded sympathetically.

'The project is due in today and they only have a library period first thing on a Friday . . . so I do hope you don't mind if I have kept them from school.'

'No, no, of course not.' Mr Paterson smiled, happily. 'Glad to know they've been doing something useful.' He turned to Douglas. 'I only called in to pick up some boxes.'

'Oh, right,' said Douglas. 'I'll give you a hand.'

He followed his father out to the hall and then carried one of the boxes of books out to the car.

'I thought we might go out for a meal tomorrow,' said Mr Paterson while they loaded the boxes into the boot. 'Do you fancy that?'

'Great,' said Douglas.

'I'll pick you up about seven.' Mr Paterson climbed into the car and strapped himself in. He paused a moment before turning the key in the ignition. 'Do all the sixth formers at your school look like her?' he asked, pointing back at the house.

'No,' said Douglas.

'Thank goodness for that,' murmured Mr Paterson, and he drove off.

It was, the boys later agreed, the speed with which Kai had acted that had been so impressive. She had been in the utility room for less than a minute but in that time she had found a shirt and tie of Douglas's in the washing basket, a skirt of his mother's, put them all on, done her hair, and come out cool as a cucumber with a story about a sociology project, computers and a free library period.

'I don't know how you had time to *think* of it all,' said Ivo, 'let alone do any of it.'

'I did not have to "think" of anything.' Kai gestured to the Touchstone that hung around her neck. 'I simply did as I was told.'

'Gedrus told you what to do?' asked Douglas.

'When you know what you want, Gedrus can tell you how to achieve it,' Kai replied. 'It is what he is for.'

It was half an hour later, and Kai was dressed in what had once been Mr Paterson's gardening clothes – a pair of jeans, a flannel shirt and a pair of wellingtons – and still managing to look rather beautiful as she stood in the hall, looking down at the boys.

'It is time to say our farewells.' She shook hands with Ivo and then turned to Douglas. 'I thank you again for your loyalty and your trust. Without your help my mission would have failed. I owe you a life debt. I may never be able to repay it but I thank you. I thank you with all my heart.'

'Will we see you again?' asked Douglas.

'I think not,' Kai smiled, a little sadly, 'but if my quest succeeds and my homeworld wins its freedom, I promise I will find some means to send you news of our victory.' She paused. 'You have the Touchstone I gave you?'

Douglas reached into his pocket for the crystal. He had been wondering when Kai would ask for it back. He knew she had only given it to him so that he could look after her while she was dead.

He held out the stone but Kai did not take it. Instead, she was fingering the stone around her own neck and looking thoughtfully down at him.

'It is of no further use to me. Or to anyone else,

apart from yourself.' She looked at him carefully. 'Would you like to keep it?'

'Well . . .' said Douglas, 'well . . . yes. I would.'

'You are sure?' Kai was still looking at him. 'The penalties for possessing one of these are severe and those that hunt me will also be hunting you. It is not a gift without risk.'

For some reason Douglas did not hesitate. 'Yes, I'm quite sure. Thank you.'

'Then use it wisely, my young friend,' Kai's hand lightly brushed his cheek as she spoke, 'and guard your secret carefully.' She stepped back and held up her arm in a salute. 'Farewell! May the Great Spirit guide you both on your journeys home.'

She turned, walked to the front door and pulled it open.

'You're sure there's nothing else you want?' said Douglas. 'I mean, if you need money or something, I could . . .'

'While I have this, I have everything I need.' Kai smiled and gestured to the stone around her neck. 'As you will discover!'

. A moment later she was striding off down the drive. She did not look back. In twenty paces she had reached the road where, without hesitation, she turned to the right and was gone.

Douglas and Ivo, standing on the front step, watched her go.

'She doesn't hang around much, does she?' said Ivo.

CHAPTER FIVE

From his office in the main building Mr Linneker was able to see the front gate, and a dark scowl crossed his face when he noticed two boys walking into school at a little after half past ten. They were ninety minutes late, he muttered to himself. Ninety minutes! But then he saw that one of the boys was Douglas, and the scowl faded.

Like most adults, Mr Linneker approved of Douglas. If Douglas was late, he knew there would be a reason. Douglas was not a boy who broke the rules without a reason. Nor was he the sort of child to shout at you over the breakfast table, refuse to do his schoolwork or get his nose pierced when you had expressly told him not to . . .

Mr Linneker sighed. He had a daughter about the same age as Douglas – in fact she was in the same class – but she was not like Douglas. Not like Douglas at all.

He walked out to the school office in time to see the two boys writing their names in the late book. 'Late again?' he asked.

'It was my fault,' said Douglas. 'I'm sorry. I had a bit of trouble at home.'

'I see.' The headmaster gave a little nod. His own parents had got divorced when he was about Douglas's age and he had some idea how difficult it could make things. 'I take it this was the same trouble as yesterday?'

'Yes,' said Douglas. 'And I asked Ivo to wait in case I needed any help. I hope that's OK?'

Mr Linneker nodded again. 'You'd better get along to class. Tell whoever's taking it that you've seen me and that it's all right.'

'Thank you.' Douglas was heading off towards the door and Ivo was about to follow, when Mr Linneker called him back.

'A word, Ivo. Before you go.'

Ivo waited, a little nervously, as his friend left the office.

'I just wanted to say,' the headmaster spoke in a low voice, 'that the support of his friends is the one thing that can make a difference for Douglas at the moment. Sticking with him this morning, being there to help if you were needed . . . You did the right thing. Well done.' Mr Linneker patted him on the shoulder. 'All right. Off you go.'

As Ivo set off down the corridor, he thought

this had definitely been the strangest day of his life.

So far this morning, he had seen a woman from another planet climb out of the bath after being dead for two days; his friend Douglas had acquired a stone that could tell you anything you wanted to know; and now, after arriving an hour and a half late for school, the headmaster had personally come out of his office to say thank you and well done. It couldn't get any stranger, he thought.

But the truth was that the *really* strange things had hardly even begun.

Douglas arrived at his history lesson to find Mr Campbell giving a test to the class on the quarrel between Henry II and Thomas à Becket. He was supposed to have revised for the test the night before but, with all the excitement of Kai and the Touch-stone, the homework had been forgotten. It occurred to him now that a librarian who knew everything might be rather useful.

He reached for the stone in his pocket and found Gedrus at his desk, playing a game of draughts.

'Hi there!' The librarian looked up with his usual greeting. 'What can I do for you?'

Douglas explained that he needed some help with the test, thinking the words in his head rather than saying them out loud, and Gedrus responded at once by hauling out a textbook identical to the one they used in class. He rattled off the answers to all twenty of the questions Mr Campbell had set and, by the end of the lesson, Douglas found himself with full marks and a gold credit on his work card.

In the Maths and French lessons that followed, it was much the same story. Gedrus not only gave the answer to any question – calculating solutions, providing vocab and correcting spelling – but, in the intervals when nothing much seemed to be happening, was available to play games.

The library had vast cupboards full of thousands of games, most of which Douglas had never heard of. He could choose any one he liked, Gedrus would throw the dice and move the pieces (in class it was easier not to draw attention to himself by reaching out a hand and doing it himself) and it was, Douglas discovered, a very pleasant way to pass the time.

Sitting in the school library at lunchtime, while Ivo was off having an accordion lesson, he started a game of Monopoly. He had just landed on Trafalgar Square and was deciding whether to buy it when a voice asked, 'D'you know anything about glaciers?'

As he let go of the Touchstone in his pocket, the image of Gedrus and the board game disappeared and he found himself facing Hannah Linneker.

Hannah had arrived in Douglas's class at the start of the term. She was a small, fierce-looking girl, with short blonde hair that stuck out in spikes from her head. She wore black lipstick, had a ring through one side of her nose – both in total defiance of school regulations – and had already been suspended twice that term by the new headmaster, who happened to be her father.

Douglas had not spoken to her before. Very few people spoke to Hannah as it was not something she encouraged. David Collins had tried to talk to her once but she had replied by pushing his head into a fire bucket and most people left Hannah alone after that. She was one of those people who always seem to be angry about something, even if all they're doing is walking down a corridor.

She was looking angry now, as she repeated her question. 'I said, do you know anything about glaciers?'

'A bit.' Douglas had done glaciers earlier in the term with Mr Phillips. 'Why?'

'I have to write this poxy essay.' Hannah waved a blank piece of paper. 'Two sides. By this afternoon.'

She looked, Douglas suddenly realized, not so much angry as very unhappy.

'I could tell you what to write,' he said cautiously. 'If you wanted.'

Hannah looked at him suspiciously. 'You could?'

'I think so.' Douglas's hand reached into his pocket and his fingers curled around the Touchstone. 'Have you got a pen?'

While Hannah retrieved a pen from her bag, he explained to Gedrus what he wanted and the librarian seemed as happy to provide an essay on glaciers

44

as to solve algebraic equations or play a game of Monopoly.

'A glacier is a slowly moving mass of ice originating in an accumulation of snow . . .' he began.

Hannah picked up her pen and started to write. In normal circumstances she did not have a lot of time for people like Douglas, who always did what they were told, always handed their work in on time and always looked so neat and clean . . . But as Douglas dictated a detailed account of the causes, origins and consequences of glaciers until she had covered exactly two sides of the paper – all without the slightest hesitation and in a little over ten minutes – she was forced to admit that, whatever else he might be, Douglas was seriously smart.

It was Ivo, at the end of the school day, who asked what he was going to do with it.

'Do with what?' said Douglas.

'The Touchstone,' said Ivo. 'If it can tell you how to get anything you want, I wondered what you were going to ask it to do.'

Douglas frowned. He had not really thought of doing anything with the Touchstone beyond playing games and getting it to do his homework. It was true that Kai had said that Gedrus could tell them how to get anything they liked but, at the moment, there was nothing in particular that he wanted.

'Only, if there wasn't anything urgent you needed

to do, and you had the time,' Ivo went on, 'I was wondering if you could ask for some help with my robot.'

Ivo's dream was to build a robot he could enter in a television programme called *Robot Wars*. In it, robots built by members of the public fought each other in an arena, battering each other with saws, spinning rotors or spring-loaded hammers until one or the other had ceased to move.

'If Gedrus is as clever as Kai says he is,' Ivo was saying, 'I thought he might be able to help. It'd be worth asking, at least.'

There was certainly no harm in asking, Douglas thought, and he reached his fingers into his pocket for the Touchstone.

'Hi there!' Gedrus was standing by his desk, juggling with five oranges. 'What can I do for you?'

'We were wondering,' said Douglas, 'if you could help Ivo build his robot. He wants to enter it in a television competition called *Robot Wars*.'

'I could probably be of some modest assistance.' Gedrus stopped juggling, letting the fruit fall neatly into the bowl on the desk. 'He wants it to look exactly like this, does he?'

To his surprise, Douglas could see that Gedrus was holding a copy of the drawing of the robot plans that Ivo had shown him on the bench at lunch break two days before.

'What did he say?' asked Ivo.

'He's got a copy of your plans and he says do you want it to look exactly like them?'

'Seriously?' A huge grin split Ivo's face. 'Tell him yes. And tell him I want . . . no!' He grabbed Douglas's arm. 'No, tell him . . .' He paused for a moment. 'Tell him I don't mind what it looks like. I just want a machine that I can build, that doesn't cost much money and that'll win. OK?'

Douglas turned to Gedrus. 'Did you hear all that?'

Gedrus nodded. 'Loud and clear.' He pulled open a drawer in the centre of his desk and took out a large roll of paper. 'I have a design here that I think might fit your needs.' He unrolled the paper on the desk, weighing down each of the corners with an orange. 'Not too expensive. You should be able to get most of the pieces from scrap and you could build it in about sixty to seventy hours. What do you think?'

The drawing on Gedrus's desk was of a rectangular box-like object on four wheels. It was complete in every detail, with some sections blown up for easier viewing and diagrams to show how the parts fitted together.

'Well?' Ivo was nudging Douglas's arm.

'He's already done it,' said Douglas. 'He's got the plans right there.'

'Already?'

'He just took them out of his desk.'

'And will it win?' asked Ivo. 'Will it win the competition?'

'I can't predict the future,' said Gedrus when Douglas relayed the question to him, 'but I've checked it against the three hundred and forty-three possible rivals and, frankly, it should wipe the floor with any of them.'

Ivo was delighted – his only frustration was that he couldn't see the plans for himself. But it turned out Gedrus had a solution to that problem as well.

If he wanted, he said, Douglas could copy them out.

When he got home Douglas spread out a large sheet of paper on the dining room table. On top of it Gedrus was able to produce a picture of the plans. The picture was only in Douglas's head of course, like the picture of the library itself, but all Douglas had to do was trace over the lines with a pen.

The plans were complicated and it was a job that would take some time, but Douglas did not mind. It was a way of saying thank you to Ivo for his help in looking after Kai and anyway, he thought, it might be quite fun to help build a robot that appeared on television and won the *Robot Wars*.

Mrs Paterson made no comment on the drawing when she finally arrived home from work at nearly six o'clock. It had been a long day at the supermarket and she was very tired. For some reason, the money in her till had not added up correctly at the end of the day and the supervisor had made her stay behind to count it again. Then, leaving the car park in a hurry, she had reversed into a bollard and broken a tail light on the car.

She was too tired to cook a proper meal and she decided they would have something very simple for supper, like baked beans on toast. Except that somehow they had run out of bread and there were no baked beans . . .

It was getting worse, she thought. Every day, it was getting worse.

Lying in bed that night Douglas reached for the Touchstone hanging round his neck under his pyjamas, and the picture of the library formed in the air above his bed.

The lighting in the library was mostly turned off and Gedrus was lying in a sleeping bag on the floor by his desk.

'Hi there!' He opened an eye to look at Douglas and yawned. 'What can I do for you?'

'I've been thinking,' said Douglas. 'You know Kai said the Guardians thought they were the only people who should have a Touchstone?'

'Yes,' Gedrus nodded.

'And you know they're trying to find anyone, like me, who's got one when they shouldn't have?'

'Mmm,' Gedrus nodded again.

'Why don't they use their Touchstones to ask where I am, and come and get me?'

'Well, they can ask,' Gedrus had propped himself up on one arm, 'but I'm not allowed to tell them. It's a privacy thing, you see. I'm not allowed to reveal anything about anyone who's got a Touchstone, unless they've told me to.'

Douglas let out a sigh of relief. If Gedrus was not allowed to tell the Guardians anything about his whereabouts, then they would not be able to find him – but there was, he realized, still a problem. Suppose a Guardian were to ask Gedrus a question like, 'Is there anyone who knows where any of the stolen Touchstones are?' What was to stop Gedrus answering, 'Yes, there is, there's Ivo Radomir and he lives at number 17 Raglan Road'? And what was to stop the Guardians from coming to interrogate him and finding Douglas that way?

The reason, when Gedrus explained it, was an interesting one, if a little complicated.

'It's an access thing,' the librarian said, sitting up in bed with his arms round his knees. 'Although everything that ever happened is held in the Great Memory, an event has to have been held in the mind of at least two conscious entities before the matrix is large enough for me to retrieve.'

What this meant, Douglas eventually understood, was that if two people witnessed an event Gedrus could describe it as if he'd been there himself, but if it was something only one person had seen the memory was too small for him to recover. As long as Ivo was the only one who knew that Douglas had a Touchstone, there was no way that Gedrus could tell the Guardians about him. Or about Ivo. It was very reassuring.

'Was there anything else?' asked Gedrus, stifling a yawn.

'One thing.' Douglas lay back on his pillow. 'I know you said building the robot wouldn't be too expensive, but how much is it going to cost exactly? Altogether?'

'Altogether . . .' Gedrus reached for a notebook on the floor beside him and opened it. 'Well, there's only a few things you'll have to buy – you'll get most of the parts from scrap – so the total outlay shouldn't be more than . . .' he ran his fingers down the page, '. . . about three hundred pounds.'

'Three hundred!' Douglas found he was speaking out loud and went back to 'talking' without moving his lips in case his mother heard. 'Where am I going to get hold of that sort of money?'

But of course Gedrus had an answer to that question as well, and Douglas was beginning to realize that was the whole point.

Gedrus had the answer to everything.

CHAPTER SIX

Mrs Paterson had taken the job at the supermarket because, now that she and Archie were separating, it didn't seem right to sit at home and do nothing. She had thought a job might give her some useful extra money, a chance to meet people and be fun, but the amount of money she earned was very small, no one she met had time to talk and the work had been no fun at all.

She had asked at the employment agency if they had any jobs that were more interesting, but the woman said no. Not for people without any exams or qualifications. At school, when her friends had been doing their GCSEs, Mrs Paterson had been ballroom dancing. In the living room she had a cabinet full of the trophies and medals she had won – including three for being Home Counties Latin American champion – but trophies in a cupboard did not count for much when it came to getting a job.

And now on top of everything else, she was increasingly worried about Douglas. He had spent all of Friday evening on his own again. First he had been in the dining room, working for almost two hours on the plans for a robot, and then he went up to his bedroom. When she went up to collect his washing, she had found him lying on his bed, his hands in his pockets, staring at the ceiling. Something was definitely wrong.

Today was Saturday and as she had the day off she had suggested they go out somewhere together, but Douglas said he wanted to finish the plans for the robot. He had been in the dining room since breakfast, sitting at the table, working busily at his drawing.

Mrs Paterson spent the morning doing housework, and was polishing the brass fittings on the front door when Hannah Linneker arrived.

She was wearing a very short black skirt, and a black T-shirt with slashes in each side that looked as if they had been made with a carving knife. As well as the black lipstick and the ring in her nose, she had a barbed wire tattoo round her upper arm and a studded leather collar round her neck.

'I've come to see Douglas,' she said.

Mrs Paterson had heard about the headmaster's daughter. Her friend, Amy Collins, said her son David had tried to speak to her once and had his face pushed into a fire bucket. The thought that this girl had somehow become a friend of Douglas was distinctly alarming.

It was always like this, she thought bitterly, as she invited Hannah inside and led her across the hall to the dining room. Just when you thought things couldn't get worse, they did.

'You've got a visitor,' she announced, before going back to her polishing.

She was careful to leave the door open as she left, in case Douglas needed to call for help.

'Do you know anything about the Black Death?' Hannah was reaching into a black plastic bag as she spoke, and taking out some papers and a pencil.

'The what?'

'The Black Death,' Hannah repeated. 'My poxy father says I have to do this poxy homework.' She sat herself the other side of the table from Douglas and spread out the paper in front of her. 'After what you did with the glaciers, I thought you could help.'

'Oh,' said Douglas. 'Right.'

Hannah had noticed before that Douglas seemed to take everything that happened to him very calmly. She had been half expecting him to say that he had better things to do than someone else's homework, but all he did was sit there and say, 'Oh. Right.'

'There's five questions and the first one is what was the poxy Black Death and how did it start.' She looked expectantly across the table.

'OK . . .' Douglas stared thoughtfully ahead of him for a moment, his hands in his pockets. 'The Black Death was an outbreak of bubonic plague that began in 1348 and is believed to have been imported to England by fleas carried on black rats . . .'

Hannah wrote down the answer as Douglas dictated it. When he had finished that question, he moved effortlessly on to saying how long the Black Death had lasted, the physical symptoms involved, how people tried to cure it and the main economic consequences.

Each answer he gave filled exactly the right amount of space on the page, he never hesitated, he never changed any words as he spoke and again, the whole thing took barely ten minutes. Hannah, though she didn't say so, was deeply impressed.

'Thanks,' she said as she stood up and put the papers and pencil back in her bag. She pointed to the plans spread out on the table. 'What's this?'

'It's the plans for a robot,' said Douglas. 'I'm building it with Ivo.'

The plans were, Hannah could see, extremely complicated. There was a mass of intricate detail and a good deal of writing, very little of which she could understand. There was an arrow pointing to one section that was 'the immodium mobilizer', there was a detailed blow-up of something called a 'linear agitator unit' and careful instructions on precautions needed to put together the 'registered pulse annotator'.

'You did all this yourself?' she asked.

'Ivo did the main design,' Douglas said modestly. 'I've just been putting in the details.'

'And you're going to build it?'

'We're starting it today,' said Douglas. 'Ivo's out at the moment getting the things we'll need, and we'll begin putting it together this afternoon.' He paused. 'You could join us if you like.'

For a brief moment Hannah was almost tempted to say yes. It was not easy, always being on her own. But then she remembered that she already had plenty of friends. They just happened to live a hundred and fifty miles away.

'I'm not really interested in robots,' she said, and she picked up her bag and left.

Ivo had had a very successful morning. Douglas had given him a list from Gedrus, of the things they would need to build the robot, with a little map of where to find them, and the mission had been more successful than he could have believed.

Pushing a wheelbarrow he had taken from home, he walked to the addresses on the list and found everything exactly where Gedrus had said it would be. The barrow was now filled with the starter motor from an abandoned car, the framework of an old go-kart he had found in a dustbin, some coils of wire that had been dumped under a hedge by the dual carriageway, and a huge assortment of scrap metal mostly taken from skips. Along with the stuff he already had in his shed, Ivo now had almost everything they would need.

He came back to Western Avenue to collect Douglas and the plans, and then the two boys pushed the wheelbarrow back to Ivo's house. The things that Gedrus said they would not need for a few days, they stored in an outhouse that had once been a coal store. Everything else, they put in the little shed at the bottom of the garden that Ivo used as a workshop.

'I suppose this is what Kai is doing,' Ivo said as he gazed happily around at the mountain of loose metal and electrical parts that covered the floor. 'Gedrus will have told her what to get and where from, and she'll be going round collecting the stuff just like we did.'

'Except she's building a spaceship,' said Douglas.

'Yes . . .' For a moment Ivo wondered if they shouldn't have been more ambitious themselves, but then realized a spaceship probably wouldn't fit in his shed. The robot was a good start, he decided. There would be time for all the other things later.

'How's she getting on?' Ivo was looking for somewhere to pin up the plans. 'Have you heard? From Gedrus?'

'He's not allowed to tell me about Kai,' said Douglas. 'It's a privacy thing. He can't reveal information about anyone who's got a Touchstone.'

'Oh.' Ivo was standing on an oil drum and pointed to length of copper tubing on the floor. 'Could you pass up that piping?'

Douglas passed it up and Ivo stacked it neatly on a shelf.

'I asked him about the money, last night, as well,' said Douglas. 'He told me that buying the last bits for the robot would cost about three hundred pounds.'

'Three hundred pounds!' Ivo nearly fell off the drum. 'Where are we going to find that sort of money?'

'It's all right,' said Douglas. 'I'm sorting it out this evening.'

Mr Paterson's car turned into the drive at exactly seven o'clock and he tooted the horn to let Douglas know he had arrived, then waited for his son to come out and join him. He preferred to wait outside when he was collecting Douglas. It meant he didn't have to meet or talk to Mrs Paterson.

They drove to an Italian restaurant – Douglas's favourite food was spaghetti – and after they had ordered, Douglas said he'd like to talk to his father about money.

'Yes, of course.' Mr Paterson reached for his wallet. 'How much do you want?'

'I wasn't really asking for any,' Douglas said. 'It's just I've got some money in my Post Office Savings book and I know it has the advantage of being very safe there and the interest is tax free so I get a gross return percentage, but it seems to me that I could get an even better return if I invested the money in stocks and shares.'

Mr Paterson blinked. It was not the sort of speech you expected to hear from a twelve year old and he hadn't realized that Douglas even knew what stocks and shares were.

'Dealing in shares can be risky,' he said eventually, 'unless you know what you're doing.'

'Yes, but you can't get the rewards without taking the risks, can you?'

It was a phrase Mr Paterson often used himself and something he fervently believed. In fact a lot of his quarrels with Mrs Paterson had been about the sort of risks they should be prepared to take with their savings.

'What I'd like to do,' Douglas went on, 'is read up about it, work out what might be a good investment, and then go to someone and tell them what shares I want to buy. I've found a financial broker . . .' he reached into his pocket and took out a piece of paper, '. . . whose office is on the way to school, but I need yours or Mum's permission before I can do anything.'

Mr Paterson did not say so, but he was impressed. His son had obviously thought the whole thing through. He had done his research, found a financial advisor, worked out a plan . . .

'What happens if you lose your money?'

'Yes.' Douglas spoke the next words very carefully. 'That's what Mum said.'

Gedrus had insisted he must use exactly those

words and had made him practise saying them several times during the day.

'You've spoken to your mother about this?'

'I asked her,' Douglas nodded, 'but she said it would be silly to take the risk.'

Mr Paterson felt a surge of annoyance. His wife had always been far too cautious about money. He hated the idea of his son growing up believing that the best thing to do with your savings was keep them in the Post Office.

'I tell you what I'll do.' Mr Paterson peered at the name on the piece of paper Douglas had given him. 'On Monday I'll go and see your Mr Parrot and if he looks honest, I'll lend you a hundred pounds to buy any shares you want. In a year's time, we'll see whether you've made a profit or not, all right?'

'That's great, Dad.' Douglas beamed across the table. 'Thanks!'

He could hardly believe it. The whole thing had been even easier than Gedrus had promised.

It was late when Douglas got home, but his mother was waiting for him in the kitchen. She was always waiting for him when he got back from being out with his father, to ask where they had been, what they had done and what they had talked about.

Douglas told her about the restaurant and what they had eaten, but did not mention buying shares or the hundred pounds. He knew his mother did not really like him going out with his father, although she never said so, and he tried not to give the impression that he had had too good a time. But these days whatever he said about his father seemed to upset her, so he usually wound up saying as little as possible.

It was only when he climbed into bed an hour later that he suddenly realized he had the answer to Ivo's question. When Ivo had asked what he was going to do with Gedrus he had not been able to say but now, he realized, he knew exactly what it was that he wanted, though he was not sure it was the sort of thing Gedrus could help him to get.

His fingers reached for the Touchstone and the librarian appeared, sitting at his desk in a dressing gown, holding a mug of cocoa.

'Hi there!' He gave Douglas a nod. 'What can I do for you?'

'I was wondering,' said Douglas, 'about my parents.'

Gedrus pursed his lips. 'What about them exactly?'

'Well, I'd like them to be back together,' said Douglas, 'like they were before. With Dad living at home like he used to. Would it be possible to make that happen?'

Gedrus scratched his ear as he considered this. 'Shouldn't be too difficult,' he said eventually. 'Take a bit of time, mind you.'

'How long?'

'A few weeks, probably.'

'A few weeks?' Douglas could not hide his astonishment. 'You can get my parents back together in a few weeks? Are you sure?'

'Can't see any real problems with that one.' Gedrus sipped his cocoa. 'As long as you do what I say.'

'And then it'll be like it was before?'

'Oh yes,' the librarian nodded. 'Exactly like it was before.'

Douglas lay back on his pillow with a deep sigh of satisfaction. That was what he really liked about Gedrus. He made even the biggest problems so *simple*.

CHAPTER SEVEN

Douglas's parents separated because of a supermarket trolley. There were other reasons as well, of course, but the trolley had been the final straw. It was the trolley that made Mr Paterson decide to leave.

Mr Paterson was a businessman. His main job was managing a garage that sold second-hand Mercedes but in his spare time he also ran a company that rented out drinks machines, and a small shop that made T-shirts with slogans on the front.

He made what most people would regard as a very good living – but it was not enough for Mr Paterson. He had always wanted not just to be well off, but to be rich. Very rich.

It was something Mrs Paterson found difficult to understand. They lived in a lovely house in one of the nicest parts of town, so why didn't they sit back and enjoy it? Why did her husband keep coming up with schemes to make more money when they had quite enough already?

Mr Paterson's latest idea had been for a new supermarket trolley. It had been invented by one of the mechanics at the garage and could steer in a straight line even when fully loaded. Mr Paterson was convinced that every supermarket in the world would want to buy it, but the idea needed money to get it started. About sixty thousand pounds, he thought. And he had suggested they raise it by mortgaging the house.

Mrs Paterson said no. If the business failed, they could lose the house. Mr Paterson pointed out that if the business succeeded, they would both be millionaires – but Mrs Paterson would not budge.

They had disagreed about such things before but this time the disagreement had been particularly painful. So painful that Mr Paterson had announced that he was leaving, and moved out.

For Douglas the change was less dramatic than for most children whose parents get a divorce. He still lived in the same house, went to the same school, and saw his father, if anything, more often than he had before. He did not like it but he accepted it. After all, there was nothing he could do about it.

Nothing, that is, until now.

'The plan,' Gedrus explained, 'is for a three-pronged attack.' He was dressed in combat fatigues and a red beret and was standing in the library beside a blackboard with 'Three-Pronged Attack' written at the top. 'One, personal appearance. Two, non-communication. And three, school. We start by getting you to look a bit scruffy – dirty shoes, un-combed hair, mud on your clothes – that sort of thing. Then you stop talking to people, except in mumbles and grunts while you're staring at the ground and looking miserable. And last, you start getting into trouble at school. You turn up late, don't hand in work on time and we generally make it clear things are going downhill.' He looked expectantly at Douglas. 'What do you think?'

'That's it?' said Douglas. 'That's all I have to do?'

'I told you it was simple.' Gedrus sat down at his desk and took out a large ring binder from one of the drawers. 'The precise details of what you'll have to do each day are in here. If we run through it together you can let me know . . .'

'How about . . .' Douglas interrupted hastily, 'you just tell me what I have to do whenever I have to do it.' It looked as if there were several thousand pages in the ring binder and he needed to get some sleep. 'I'm sure whatever you've worked out is going to be fine.'

'Well,' Gedrus looked suitably modest as he closed the ring binder and returned it to the drawer, 'I think it'll do the job.'

Ivo, when Douglas told him about it the next morn-ing, was less convinced. He said he could not see how being untidy, mumbling a lot and turning up late for school could get anyone's parents back together.

'The point is to make them feel guilty,' Douglas explained as they sat on the battered sofa in Ivo's shed. 'Gedrus says if I can make them think that splitting up is causing me a deep emotional trauma, eventually they'll feel so bad they'll want to go back to how they were.'

Ivo frowned. 'When do you start?' he asked.

'I've started already.' Douglas pointed to a mud splash on his trousers. 'And I'm going to stay here all day if that's all right. Gedrus says if I'm out all day, it'll make Mum worry about me and then when I go home and she asks what I've been doing I won't tell her and she'll worry even more.'

Ivo was still doubtful, but if it meant Douglas would spend the whole day in Raglan Road helping to build the robot, he certainly wasn't going to argue.

Building the robot turned out to be something they both enjoyed. Ivo did most of the practical work while Douglas provided, through Gedrus, the instructions on what should be done – and the wonderful thing about having Gedrus to help was that you never had to sit and wonder what to do next. Gedrus told you. He always knew exactly what piece to fit next. He knew where it was and how to cut it to the right size. He knew what spanner you would need to fit it and where you'd left it. With Gedrus in charge there was never a wasted second. And the result was that progress was extraordinarily fast. Ivo could not have been more pleased.

When Mrs Radomir finally came in and told them it was time to pack up, Ivo asked Douglas if he would be able to come round the following day after school and do some more.

'I'm planning to come round every evening next week,' Douglas replied. 'Gedrus says it's important to keep Mum worrying about why I don't want to be at home, but on Monday I might be a little late.'

On Monday after school, he explained, he had an appointment to see Mr Parrot.

Mr Parrot's office was on the top floor of a tall, narrow building in Castle Street. It was a small office and the financial advisor himself was a big man, with a large, round body that only just fitted behind his desk. Above him the roof sloped inwards so steeply that, when he stood up to welcome Douglas, he had to lean forward to avoid bumping his head on the ceiling.

'I talked to your father this morning,' he said. With a podgy hand, he motioned Douglas, who seemed to have a large food stain down one side of his shirt, to a chair. 'He told me you wanted to invest some of your savings in shares.' Mr Parrot smiled approvingly. 'Very sensible. Did you have any particular stocks in mind?'

'Yes. I'd like to put a hundred pounds in the Travers Mining Company, please,' said Douglas.

Mr Parrot had never heard of the Travers Mining Company but he looked them up on his computer.

'Ah . . .' His smile faded. 'I wouldn't advise getting involved in that one. It's a gold mining company in Canada and hasn't registered a profit since 1973.'

'I know, but those are the shares I want to buy.' Douglas took out his calculator. 'I've worked out that, for a hundred pounds, you should be able to get three hundred and forty-five shares, including your commission.'

Mr Parrot leaned his bulky frame over the desk. 'If it hasn't made a profit in thirty years, it's not likely to make one now, you know. My advice would be to . . .'

'Thank you,' Douglas interrupted him. 'But those are the only shares I want to buy.'

When Mr Paterson had called into the office earlier in the day, his instructions to Mr Parrot had been very specific. He said he wanted his son to be encouraged to make his own decisions even if it meant losing his money. Being prepared to make a gamble and learn from it, he said, was a lesson we all had to learn.

'Well, it's your decision.' Mr Parrot tapped on the desk with his pencil for a moment. 'You're quite sure you don't want to hear any other suggestions?'

'It's very kind of you,' said Douglas, 'but no.'

Mr Parrot watched Douglas leave and sighed. He liked his work but some days it felt like an uphill struggle.

Half an hour later, however, he was astonished to

notice on his computer read-out of the latest market reports, an announcement by the board of the Travers Mining Company of the discovery of a large deposit of bauxite on their territory. As a result, their shares had jumped to three pounds fifty each, and were still climbing. The stock he had bought for Douglas twenty minutes before was now worth well over a thousand pounds.

Mr Parrot rather wished he had bought some of the shares for himself.

In his bedroom that night Douglas held the Touchstone as it lay on his chest under his shirt. He had recently discovered that the picture of Gedrus and the library did not always have to be exactly a metre-wide square. If he asked, Gedrus could make the picture larger or smaller or, as he had done now, expand it so that it filled his entire vision.

To Douglas, although he knew he was still sitting in his bedroom at home, it felt as if he was actually in the library with Gedrus, surrounded by bookshelves. The librarian himself was at his desk doing a jigsaw of the *Flying Scotsman* by the soft light of a table lamp.

'I wanted to ask,' said Douglas, 'how you knew those mining shares would suddenly be worth so much more?'

'It was very simple.' Gedrus studied the lid of the jigsaw box before putting another piece into place. 'The company did a geological survey a month ago and the report was delivered to the board last Wednesday. The size of the bauxite deposit meant they had to make money.'

As he spoke, the area to the right of the librarian's desk was suddenly filled with a group of men in suits, sitting round a long mahogany table. At the far end one man was talking enthusiastically, pointing to a map as he spoke.

'What's that?' asked Douglas. 'What's happening?'

'That's the surveyor giving his report to the board,' Gedrus answered without looking up from his puzzle. 'I thought you might like a visual display. You can have the sound as well, if you like.'

Douglas walked over to the office scene and stared at the group of men as they listened attentively to the surveyor. 'This is what actually happened? This is them having the meeting?'

'If you don't want it,' Gedrus had got up from the desk and walked over to join him, 'I'll get rid of them.'

'No! No, I don't want you to . . .' Douglas paused. 'Does that mean you can show me anything? Anything that's ever happened? In the world?'

'In the galaxy.' Gedrus gave him a mildly reproving look. 'I keep telling you, it's a very big library.'

'You can show me anything?' said Douglas. 'Anything at all? Like . . . if I wanted to see what I was doing on my sixth birthday, you could show me that?'

The men round the table disappeared and were instantly replaced by a kitchen. It was the kitchen from his old house, Douglas realized, before they moved, and directly in front of him, sitting at the head of the table with a party hat on his head was a boy he recognized as himself, at six years old. His friend Paul, who had moved to Australia, was sitting on his right, looking impossibly small, his eyes wide and shining. There were half a dozen other faces gathered round the table, eating, laughing . . . and at the far end were his parents, his father with his arm round his mother's waist, smiling happily.

If he reached out his hand he could touch any one of them. It was as if he were a ghost, haunting his own past.

'If you'd rather see a different bit of the day, you've only to say.' Gedrus had come over to stand beside Douglas, his hands thrust deep into his pockets, gazing out at the scene before them.

It didn't stop, thought Douglas. Right from the start, it had never stopped.

The whole thing just got more and more amazing.

CHAPTER EIGHT

For Douglas, it was the start of one of the most extraordinary and exciting times of his life. When Gedrus had shown him his sixth birthday, he had finally begun to comprehend the almost unimaginable size of the library at his command, and it changed everything.

The librarian could show him whatever he wanted to see. Gedrus could take him to a million planets circling round a million different suns. He could show him the civilizations that had risen there and died. He could tell him stories that spanned a billion years and thousands of civilizations, more stories than Douglas could ever know about even if all he did was sit and read their titles between now and the day he died. And to see them, all he had to do was ask. At school or at home, all he had to do was touch the stone and he could be, literally, in another world.

There were so many choices that usually he would let Gedrus do the choosing, and the stories that Gedrus most frequently told and the ones Douglas liked best, were stories about the Touchstones – perhaps because they helped him understand a little more about the extraordinary object that had fallen into his possession.

Gedrus showed Douglas how, three million years before, a race called the Yōb had discovered how to access the Great Memory, that place within the folds of time where everything that ever happened is held and stored. He showed him how the first Touchstones had been made, in a process that no other race had been able to repeat because making a Touchstone, like finding the Holy Grail, could only be achieved by *being* a particular sort of person.

He showed how every Yōbian on a thousand planets had once owned a Touchstone and what it had meant to them and the glories that their civilization had achieved. He showed Douglas the great buildings in which they lived, the huge ships in which they travelled between the stars. And he told the story of how the Yōb had suddenly disappeared in a single night, all of them, no one knew where, leaving only empty cities and towns to crumble over the millennia into dust.

He showed Douglas how a Denebian scout ship, exploring one of these ruins – at a time when humans on earth were hunting mammoths with bows and arrows – had found a cache of several hundred Touch-stones, all unused. A member of the crew had picked one of them up and, like Douglas, discovered what they could do.

Long and terrible wars had been fought for owner-ship of those stones and Gedrus showed them as well. He showed the story of the desperate search among the ruins of all the Yōbian worlds for other caches and more unused Touchstones. And then the story of how the Touchstones had gradually come under the control of the Guardians. Only the Guardians were allowed to possess a Touchstone. Only the Guardians could say how they should be used, and where. And once the Guardians controlled the stones, they came to control the Federation. Under their iron fist a peace had been restored throughout the galaxy and their power and authority had only grown over the millennia.

Douglas listened to these stories whenever he could. In bed at night, in the evenings round at Ivo's shed and, most peacefully, in his lessons at school dur-ing the day. They were a lot more interesting than Mr Phillips droning on about beef production in the Argentine or Mr Campbell talking about the medieval wool trade, and it didn't matter if his teachers noticed that he wasn't really paying attention to the lesson. Looking as if he wasn't paying attention was part of the plan to get his parents back together anyway.

In the evening after school, he would walk round to

Ivo's house, where the robot they were building came together with astonishing speed. The boys worked on it every evening and most of the weekends. Ivo would have worked on it all through the night if he had been able to. Most of the time they had no idea how what they were building would work, but it didn't seem to matter. Gedrus knew what he was doing and that was enough.

In a little over a fortnight they were ready to give the robot its first test run. They called it the *Indestructible* because Gedrus told them that's what it was and though it did not look particularly exciting – it was a steel box about a metre long and half a metre wide – it did not behave like any other robot they had seen.

Surrounded by what Gedrus told them was a Tenebrian force field, you could have hit it with a ten-ton sledgehammer and not made it move a millimetre or even dented its surface. With the field turned on nothing could touch it. Yet when you set it going, as Ivo did, and ran it at a paving slab propped up on the grass by a couple of pegs, it smashed its way through the stone as if it were tissue paper. In the *Robot Wars* arena nothing was going to touch it. Nothing.

Ivo was ecstatic, though he did ask for one change to the design. However unnecessary in the practical sense, he felt the *Indestructible* should have some sort of weapon, like the hammers, circular saws or flamethrowers of other robots. Gedrus, when Douglas asked if this would be possible, produced plans for a device called a Nihilator, that could be mounted on top of the robot. It would, he said, generate a plasma vortex that disrupted the molecular stability of anything it was aimed at. Neither of the boys had the least idea what this meant but it sounded, as Ivo said, pretty cool.

The librarian warned the boys that building it would cost more money but by that time money was no longer a problem.

These days, when Douglas climbed the five flights of stairs to Mr Parrot's office he was given a most enthusiastic welcome. Mr Parrot would heave his huge bulk up from his chair, shake Douglas warmly by the hand and show him to a seat. He made no mention of his young client's increasingly untidy appearance, but offered him a chocolate biscuit, a can of drink from the fridge, and then listened carefully and attentively while Douglas explained what shares he would like to buy next.

He no longer made any attempt to dissuade him from buying into companies that looked, on paper, to be incapable of making a profit. If Douglas said shares were worth buying then they were. There was no argument.

Shares in the Travers Mining Company had gone up to six pounds before Mr Parrot sold them the following day. Douglas had then invested the money in a dot.com company that helped people find the cheapest travel fares. Those shares had quadrupled in value before the end of the week. After that there had been a Swiss pharmaceutical company and a firm of Cambridge software designers – both turning in huge profits within a day or two of Douglas buying their shares.

It seemed that whatever Douglas touched made a profit and after only two weeks, the value of his investments stood at a little over a quarter of a million pounds. Mr Parrot, to judge by his new suit and the news that he was planning to move to a suite of larger offices in the centre of town, had made a fair amount of money for himself as well. So it was not surprising that he smiled when he saw Douglas arrive, though on one occasion he did express a certain concern.

'I hope you won't mind,' he said after Douglas had told him he wanted to invest in the Swiss company working on a pill that could make people thin, 'but I have to ask. How do you know which shares are worth buying?' He looked apologetically at Douglas before going on. 'I'm legally obliged, you see, to take all reasonable precautions to ensure that you're not breaking the law and your success is not the result of inside information.'

Douglas said he didn't know what inside information was.

'It's when you know someone inside the company,' Mr Parrot explained, 'who tells you something that the rest of the public don't know. Has anyone been doing anything like that?'

Douglas thought about it and decided he could honestly say that no one in any of the companies in which he had bought shares had ever told him anything.

'No,' he said.

'So how do you know which companies are going to be successful?'

'Well,' said Douglas carefully, 'I get these sort of pictures in my head. They tell me what shares to buy, and I tell you.'

Mr Parrot gave a big sigh of relief. It was exactly the answer he had been hoping for. He had read a story once about a boy who had been able to predict the winners in horse races by seeing their names in his head while he was sitting on a rocking horse. Douglas obviously had a similar ability.

'Is that all right?' asked Douglas. 'It's not breaking the law or anything?'

'It's not breaking the law,' said Mr Parrot firmly, 'and it's very all right. You feel free to come and tell me about your pictures any time. Any time at all.'

It was all was going better than Douglas could ever have imagined. His days passed in a glorious routine of watching the vast spectacle of galactic history provided by Gedrus, and robot building with Ivo. And as if all that were not enough, Gedrus was at the same time telling him how to achieve the only other thing he wanted – how to bring his parents back together.

Putting Gedrus's plan into practice had, at first, been rather more difficult than Douglas had expected. When Gedrus told him that over the coming days he should let his appearance become increasingly untidy, it sounded simple enough – but unfortunately Douglas was the sort of person who straightened his tie and tucked his shirt in several times a day without thinking. He would carefully disarrange his clothes before he left for school and then find he had unconsciously combed his hair and brushed the dirt from his blazer before he even arrived.

Again, Gedrus told Douglas that when teachers spoke to him he was not to reply directly but stare at his feet, mumble his answers and occasionally not answer at all. The trouble was that Douglas liked most of his teachers, and when they put a hand on his shoulder and asked how things were going, he would find himself smiling back and saying a polite, 'Not too bad, thank you', before he could stop himself.

He did manage to be late for class occasionally but even this did not have the effect he expected. Douglas had never been any trouble in the past and teachers presumed, as Mr Linneker had, that when he was late there was probably some good reason. Most of them knew about his parents and when he walked in the door, they would nod understandingly and tell him to go and sit down.

Help came, in the end, from a quite unexpected quarter. Hannah Linneker knew a lot about behaving badly at school. Hannah could annoy teachers just by being in the same room, and it was when she began telling Douglas what to do that things really started to happen.

It was Hannah who taught Douglas how to walk with that sort of scuffling slouch that drives all adults mad. How to keep his face a mask and never show any emotion, in particular never to smile. And it was Hannah who put gel in his hair to make it stick up at funny angles and explained about making sure he never had the right pencil or the right book for a class.

It was Hannah who told him how to wear his tie with the knot too tight and out of place but not quite out of place enough for a teacher to complain. She told him how to look as if he was thinking of an answer when he was asked a question, but then let the silence grow and never actually say anything. The two of them sat together at the back of the class, carefully practising the sort of bored disinterested look that was guaranteed to annoy even the most sympathetic and supportive teacher.

And in return for her help Douglas did most of Hannah's schoolwork – either asking Gedrus to dictate the answers she needed or simply letting her copy the answers from his own exercise books.

It was an arrangement that benefited both of them.

Douglas had been puzzled at first, since Hannah cared so little about school, that she bothered to do the work at all, but it turned out there was a reason. Before becoming headmaster, Mr Linneker had been deputy head of a school in Norwich. That was where Hannah had left all her friends and her father had said he would allow her to go back and see them over half term, but only if her schoolwork was satisfactory. And with Douglas's help, her schoolwork was proving to be very satisfactory indeed.

At the same time reports were filtering back to Mr Linneker that Douglas Paterson had changed, that he was no longer the tidy, attentive pupil he used to be, and that his attitude in class had become a cause for concern. It was only a matter of time, Gedrus said happily, before the news got back to his parents.

Mrs Paterson was worried about Douglas long before she heard reports of his behaviour at school. In the last two weeks her son seemed to have become a recluse. He never saw any of his old friends. If he wasn't round at Ivo's he would sit for hours in his bedroom, staring at the wall in front of him without uttering a word. He hardly spoke to her at all. What had happened to the serene and sunny child who had delighted her life for the last twelve years, she had no idea, nor what she should do about it.

She rang Mr Paterson, who told her she was exaggerating, and then she rang the school, who arranged for both parents to come in and talk to the headmaster. It was not a comfortable meeting. Mr Linneker began by telling them, in some detail, how Douglas's behaviour, attitude and appearance had become a cause for serious concern. Mrs Paterson was soon crying. Mr Paterson said he couldn't understand why his son's personality had changed so dramatically, and Mr Linneker said you didn't have to be a rocket scientist to realize that a twelve-year-old boy is bound to be unsettled when his parents decide to get divorced.

It had, said Gedrus, gone better than he thought possible, and he calculated it was only a question of time before Mr Paterson moved back into the house in Western Avenue.

Douglas ought to have been delighted at the news but somehow he wasn't. Gedrus had shown him the entire meeting as he walked home from school and the more he saw of his mother's distress and his father's pale, strained face, the more he wondered if the whole thing had been quite such a good idea.

The librarian had no such reservations. 'You couldn't have asked for it to go better than that,' he said as he hopped up and down the library on a pogo stick. 'I'm telling you, we've got them on the run now.'

'But they looked so unhappy,' said Douglas. 'I didn't want to make them unhappy.'

'Unhappy was the whole point of the plan, Doug!' Gedrus bounced enthusiastically round his desk. 'We had to make your dad feel so bad about leaving that he'd change his mind and come back.'

'I didn't want to make him feel bad either.'

'Douglas! The *plan* was to make him feel bad. I told you that at the start.'

This was, Douglas had to admit, quite true.

'And it's working brilliantly,' Gedrus went on. 'Another couple of weeks and we'll have him back in the house, I promise.'

That thought, at least, made Douglas feel a bit better. 'Well, I suppose it's worth it. If it means they'll be happy in the long run.'

'Happy?' Gedrus paused in mid-bounce.

'Yes. When we're all back in the same house, happy together, it won't matter that . . .'

'My memory,' Gedrus did not often interrupt when Douglas was talking, but he did now, 'is that the point of this operation was to get things back to the way they were before. No one said anything to me about people being happy.'

'But . . .' for a moment Douglas suddenly felt his whole world slipping sideways, 'but that was the whole reason I was doing it.'

'You never said anything about making anyone happy,' Gedrus repeated stubbornly. 'You said you wanted to make things like they were before and that's what I've been telling you how to do.'

There was an empty feeling in Douglas's stomach. What the librarian said was perfectly true. That was exactly what he had said, and it was no good complaining that he had meant something different. Gedrus had answered exactly the question he had been asked, and Douglas had only himself to blame if he had asked the wrong question.

'You're saying my parents were unhappy before?' he said, his voice no more than a whisper.

'Of course they were unhappy before!' Gedrus had resumed his bouncing. 'That's why they were getting divorced.'

'And if Dad moves back in, they're going to be unhappy again?'

'Absolutely miserable, I'd say,' said Gedrus.

And it was after that, that all sorts of things started going seriously pear-shaped.

CHAPTER NINE

Douglas wanted to tell Ivo how the plan to bring his parents together had gone wrong – but when he walked round to Ivo's house he found the street filled with an ambulance, two police cars, an electricity van and a fire engine.

A small crowd had gathered on the pavement and, while everyone knew there had been some sort of accident, nobody was quite sure what it was. One woman said she'd heard a young boy had been electrocuted by a falling power line, someone else thought Mrs Radomir had been crushed by a falling tree, but the policeman standing outside the door to number 17 would not say if either of these stories was true. Nor would he let Douglas inside to find out.

A few minutes later, however, to Douglas's great relief, Ivo was wheeled out of the house by two ambulance men, with a large dressing on the side of his head, but smiling and looking very much alive. He had a chance for a quick word with Douglas before he was put into the ambulance.

'It was all my fault.' He spoke in a low voice, so that no one else could hear. 'I got the range wrong.'

'The range? What range?'

'On the Nihilator.' Ivo looked slightly embarrassed. 'I hit a telegraph pole. I should have waited for you.'

'Are you all right?'

'I'm fine.' The men were lifting Ivo into the ambulance and he gave Douglas a wave. 'I'll call you this evening. Tell you all about it . . .'

In fact Douglas did not have to wait for Ivo's call to find out what had happened. He got the story from Gedrus while he was walking home, though the librarian was careful to say he was only deducing what had probably happened as Ivo had been on his own at the time.

Using the plans Douglas had made for him, Ivo had finished the Nihilator when he got home from school and, instead of waiting for Douglas to join him, had decided to try out the weapon on his own. He set up a tin can at one end of the workbench in his shed and fired at it. The can was destroyed in a very satisfying manner – it simply disappeared – but so was half the shed wall and the base of the telegraph pole two metres behind it. Meanwhile, the recoil from firing the weapon sent Ivo flying backwards through the door. Though painful, it was this that saved his life. A moment later, the top ten metres of the telegraph pole fell directly on to the shed, smashing it to matchwood. If Ivo had been inside he would have been killed outright.

It had been a narrow escape but, Douglas realized, there was now a fresh danger facing them both. The authorities would want to know why the telegraph pole had fallen down. They would investigate, they would ask questions, and if they found the accident had been caused by two twelve year olds building a plasma vortex generator, the consequences would be more serious than a slapped wrist and stopped pocket money.

He remembered Kai's warning that he should guard his secret carefully, and how Gedrus had told him on more than one occasion that it was only if no one else knew about the Touchstone that he would be able to keep it. The Guardians wanted it back. They had been searching for it ever since it was stolen. They might not be able to ask Gedrus directly where it was but there were other questions they could ask.

They could ask if anyone knew of someone who had displayed unusual abilities recently . . . or shown an exceptional knowledge of technology. An item in the national news about two twelve-year-old boys with a Nihilator and a Tenebrian force field would be like a beacon telling them where to find at least one of the missing Touchstones.

And if the police found the *Indestructible* or the

Nihilator it certainly *would* be national news, though Gedrus thought there was no immediate danger of discovery. The *Indestructible* was safely out of sight in the outhouse, where Ivo had stored it to make room in the shed and, despite his injuries, he had managed to hide the Nihilator in some long grass before the ambulance men took him away. But the librarian did confirm that if the authorities found either the robot or the weapon, the consequences would be disastrous.

'It's exactly the sort of clue the Guardians are looking for,' he explained cheerily, sitting at his desk in the library, eating an ice cream. 'Anyone gets to see either of those things in action and you'll have a squadron of Federation Special Forces round your ears before you can say oops!'

Since the whole purpose of building the robot and its weapon had been to let everyone see them in action on television, Douglas felt that the librarian might have warned them about this earlier. But it was an argument he thought he would save until later. The first thing to do was make sure the *Indestructible* was hidden somewhere safe. Gedrus said that an investigator from British Telecom would be round the next morning to try and find out why one of his telegraph poles had collapsed so mysteriously. He must not be allowed to stumble on the truth.

Gedrus thought Ivo would probably be released from hospital that evening, in which case he would be able to hide the robot, but there was a chance they might keep him in overnight, in which case Douglas would somehow have to do it himself.

Worried, Douglas was not in the mood to talk much when he got home. His mother was very quiet as well. She was already in the kitchen cooking supper when he got in but she said nothing about him being late, or about her meeting in school with Mr Linneker earlier that day. In fact she hardly spoke a word throughout the meal, even when Douglas told her about Ivo's accident.

Mr Paterson rang while they were doing the washing-up. He was calling from the airport, on his way to a car fair in Stuttgart, and said that he wanted a serious talk with Douglas when he got back on Sunday evening. He had a brief word with Mrs Paterson who came back to the kitchen looking as if she had been crying again. They finished the dishes in silence and then Douglas went up to his room.

Ivo phoned later in the evening to say he was home from the hospital. His right foot was in plaster, he had fourteen stitches in the cut on his head and he would be off school the next day – but otherwise he seemed very cheerful. When Douglas told him what Gedrus had said about not letting anyone find the robot or the Nihilator, he promised to make sure they were both safely hidden before the BT investigator arrived the next day. It was only when Douglas went on to explain why they would never be able to enter the *Robot Wars* that he went rather quiet. Douglas could tell how upset he was at the news. Much more upset about that than about breaking a bone in his ankle.

When Douglas finally got to bed that night he found it difficult to sleep. He was feeling thoroughly depressed and he lay there in the dark, listening to the sound of the rumba coming from the drawing room downstairs.

It went on for hours.

At school the next morning, it got worse. Miss Rattle asked Douglas to wait behind at the end of registration. She was Douglas's form tutor, but also took him for maths.

'I've marked the test you did yesterday,' she told him, 'and you scored one out of twenty.'

She held out his exercise book and Douglas stared at it.

'Are you sure?'

'You can check to see if I've made any mistakes.' Miss Rattle was reaching for a piece of paper on her desk. 'Rather more serious is the fact that you only scored four per cent on the exam we did on Tuesday.'

'Four per cent!' Douglas looked at her in disbelief. All his answers had been provided by Gedrus, and it was hard to believe the galactic librarian had failed to cope with a maths exam for twelve year olds.

'Mr Harris tells me you did equally badly in his science quiz on Wednesday.'

The science quiz was another test to which Gedrus had provided all the answers. Douglas couldn't understand it.

'I know you've been having problems at home,' Miss Rattle went on, 'but I really can't accept this work. I've asked Mr Linneker to talk to you about it. He's waiting for you in his office.'

As he left the classroom Douglas reached for the Touchstone under his shirt. 'What's happening?' he demanded.

Gedrus was hitting a tennis ball against an empty section of the wall on one side of the library. 'Happening? Where?'

'This maths exam!' Douglas waved his exam paper. 'I got four per cent! You told me what to write and I got four per cent! You gave me the wrong answers!'

'I know.' Gedrus flicked the ball with a neat backhand pass. 'It was the next part of the plan.'

'What plan?'

'The plan to get your parents worried about you, so that your father would move back into the house. The last couple of days I've been letting your work get worse to show you didn't care about it.'

'And you didn't tell me?'

'If you remember,' said Gedrus, pulling a large ring binder from a drawer in the desk, 'I asked at the beginning if you wanted to be informed of all the details of the plan but you said no. You only wanted to be told what you had to do next.'

Douglas remembered that two weeks before, he had said exactly this, but it didn't stop him feeling distinctly aggrieved. Grimly he walked down the corridor to the headmaster's office wondering as he went, how someone with all the knowledge in the universe could be so incredibly stupid.

When he arrived at Mr Linneker's office, he found the headmaster sitting at his desk, staring out of the window. He seemed to have some difficulty remembering who Douglas was.

'Yes?' he said eventually. 'What is it?'

'Miss Rattle told me to come and see you,' said Douglas. 'About my maths.'

'Oh yes.' Mr Linneker nodded vaguely. 'You didn't do very well, did you?'

'No,' said Douglas.

Mr Linneker picked up a teaspoon, took a spoonful of paperclips and slowly stirred them into a cup of tea on his desk. 'Perhaps you could . . . try and do a bit better next time.'

Douglas said that he would, Mr Linneker nodded, and silence descended again.

'Is that all?' said Douglas, eventually.

'What?' Mr Linneker seemed to be surprised he was still there. 'Oh, yes, that's all.' As Douglas got up and walked to the door, the headmaster suddenly added, 'You haven't seen Hannah, have you? Today, I mean?'

'Hannah?' Douglas shook his head. 'No.'

'No.' The headmaster nodded. 'It was just a

thought. I know you've been quite friendly with her recently. For which I'm very grateful.'

'Is something wrong?' said Douglas but Mr Linneker did not seem to hear. He was staring out of the window again, lost in thought.

Out in the corridor Douglas asked Gedrus why the headmaster was behaving so strangely.

'It's Hannah,' said Gedrus. 'She's run away from home.'

'Run away? Why? Where did she go?'

'She's trying to get to Norwich.' Gedrus was standing by his desk, pointing at a large map of Britain pinned up on a board. 'She left home last night after a big row with her father, got a train to London this morning and, at the moment, she's sitting on a bench at Paddington Station.'

'What was the row about?' asked Douglas. He had a nasty feeling that he already knew, but he had to be sure.

'Her father said she could go to Norwich at half term,' said Gedrus, 'as long as her schoolwork was satisfactory. But her marks in some recent tests have been so bad that he said she couldn't go.'

And Douglas knew exactly why Hannah's marks had been so bad. Sitting together at the back of the class, she had copied all her answers from him.

It had all gone wrong. Everything had gone terribly wrong. He had wanted to bring his parents back together and only succceded in making both of them miserable. He had helped his best friend build a machine that not only destroyed his precious workshop, but very nearly got him killed. He had thought he was helping Hannah with her work by letting her copy his answers but all he had done was get her into even more trouble, and now she had run away from home.

He had wanted to make everything better – and he could hardly have made things worse if he'd tried.

The only thing that had gone right since Kai gave him the Touchstone was the money, and it looked for a moment as if he had lost that as well.

Douglas called in on Mr Parrot on his way home from school the next day and found the financial advisor on the landing outside his office talking to a man in white overalls who was fitting a new lock to the door.

'We had a burglary at lunch time,' Mr Parrot told Douglas, a worried look on his normally smiling face. 'I must say, I'll be glad when I get to the new office. Proper security there.'

'They haven't stolen my money, have they?' asked Douglas.

'No, no, nothing to worry about on that score.' Mr Parrot sat his young client down with a plate of Jaffa cakes and then squeezed behind the desk to his own chair. 'Nothing stolen as far as we can see, not even the computer. Which is rather odd.'

On a happier note, Mr Parrot went on to say that Douglas's shares in the Malawi automobile company had doubled overnight with the announcement of a takeover bid. And when Douglas told him to sell them and buy stock in a Chinese company that made X-ray machines for hospitals, his whole body shook as he chuckled with pleasure.

'Your father's going to find all this as hard to believe as I do,' he said, carefully noting down the name of the company.

'I . . . I thought we weren't going to tell him,' said Douglas.

'Not at the moment, certainly,' Mr Parrot gave Douglas an encouraging smile, 'but I promised to give him a report every three months. I don't think it's something you have to worry about. I promise you, he's going to be very pleased!'

But Douglas did worry. As he walked home, the thought of explaining to his parents how he had come by half a million pounds suddenly seemed rather daunting. Mr Parrot might have been happy with the story about Douglas getting pictures in his head, but he was not sure his parents would believe it so easily. They would want to know the truth, and the truth was the one thing he couldn't tell them. He had thought that having Gedrus would make everything so simple but, wherever he looked, it only seemed to make things more complicated.

At home he noticed a strange car parked in the

drive and wondered if someone had brought his mother home early from the supermarket.

'Mum?' he called as he let himself in the front door. 'Are you home?'

There was no answer, but he could hear someone moving in the living room. There was the clink of china, followed by the noise of someone clearing their throat. Douglas crossed the hall to the living room and pushed open the door.

On the far side of the room, standing with his back to the fireplace, was a short, round man with a shiny round head that was almost entirely bald. He wore a dark three-piece suit, small rimless glasses under white, bushy eyebrows, and was holding a cup of tea in one hand. He frowned slightly as Douglas came into the room.

'Ah, Douglas.' He put down the cup and saucer on the mantelpiece. 'At last.'

'Who are you?' asked Douglas, but of course he already knew. He had known as soon as he had seen the green stone that the man was lightly fingering as it hung on a silver chain around his neck.

It had happened.

Somehow, in a little less than three weeks, the Guardians had found him.

CHAPTER TEN

The Guardian was not, at first glance, a particularly frightening figure. His suit was crumpled, his glasses had slipped down his nose and he had the sort of tired, harassed look that teachers get when they're trying to check everyone is back on the coach at the end of a long school trip.

None of which stopped Douglas feeling more frightened than he had ever been in his life. He knew a little about the Guardians from Gedrus. Under galactic law, the man in front of him had the right to turn him into a protein fluid and drink him as soup.

'My name is Quomp,' said the man. 'I am a Guardian from the Federation's Seventeenth Quadrant and I believe you have something that doesn't belong to you.'

He held out his hand and waited while Douglas took the chain from round his neck and dropped the

Touchstone into his outstretched palm.

'Thank you.' The Guardian put the stone into the pocket of his jacket. 'Now, we have a lot to talk about so I suggest you sit down.' He motioned Douglas to a chair. 'First I need to know who gave this to you, when, and everything that's happened since. Start at the beginning and don't miss anything out.'

Douglas would have liked to reply but he found when he opened his mouth to speak, that no sound came out.

'All right, all right . . .' the Guardian did not seem too upset by the silence, '. . . we'll try it a different way. I'll tell you what I think happened and you tell me if I've got it right.' His hands clasped behind his back, he began pacing up and down in front of the fireplace. 'Three weeks ago four Touchstones were stolen from a Federation Survey vessel on Patka by a Vangarian warrior named Kai Akka Kahkousi. She escaped, but in the process both she and her ship were so badly damaged that she was forced to make an emergency landing on a prohibited planet and hide while her body regenerated.

'My guess would be,' the Guardian paused to pick up his tea from the mantelpiece, 'that she came here, told you she was an alien from another planet and asked for your help. To convince you she was who she said she was and to make sure you knew how to look after her during regeneration, she gave you one of the Touchstones. You looked after her, she recovered and, when she left to organize some means of getting back to her home planet, she let you keep the stone, probably as a way of making sure you didn't tell anyone what had happened.'

He lowered his nose into his tea, took a deep breath and sucked up the entire contents of the cup with a deep gurgling noise. Then he took out a handkerchief, mopped the end of his nose and looked across at Douglas. 'Would that be a fair summary?'

Douglas nodded.

'Well . . .' The Guardian put down his cup. 'What we have to do now is catch her and get the other stones back before she gets home and starts a major war. It's not going to be easy but Gedrus says we have a chance, if you'll help.'

'Help?' Douglas finally managed to speak, though his voice sounded thin and high.

'I can't promise it won't be dangerous,' Quomp looked at Douglas over the top of his glasses, 'but as long as you do exactly as I tell you, you should be all right.'

'You want me to help you catch Kai?'

'I think in the circumstances it's the least you can do.' The Guardian gave Douglas a reproving look. 'I mean, if you hadn't agreed to hide her we wouldn't have this problem in the first place, would we? She'd be safely under lock and key and we could all be at home with our feet up watching television.'

'But . . .' Douglas hesitated. The conversation

was not going quite as he had expected. 'But Kai was trying to win a war to free her people.'

The Guardian frowned. 'Yes?'

'Her planet is ruled by a tyrant and she needed the Touchstone to overthrow him. She told me.'

Quomp gave a little sigh. 'Oh dear.' He sat down in an armchair. 'You're telling me you decided to help her because what she was doing was right?'

'Well, yes,' said Douglas. 'I checked with Gedrus. He said everything she told me was the truth.'

'I'm sure he did.' The Guardian took off his glasses and pinched the bridge of his nose. There was a pause while he fingered the Touchstone round his neck before he went on. 'Perhaps I could persuade you that there is another way of looking at this. May I try?'

'Do I have a choice?' asked Douglas.

The Guardian of the Federation's Seventeenth Quadrant considered this for a moment, then shook his head. 'No,' he said. 'Not really.'

Ivo had not had an easy day. His head was throbbing from the cut on his temple, his ribs ached and his foot, encased in plaster, hurt whenever he moved it – but these were not the things that bothered him most.

That morning the engineer from British Telecom had arrived at the house and he told Mrs Radomir it was his job to discover exactly why the telegraph pole had fallen down the day before. Ivo watched from the bedroom window as the man poked carefully through the remains of the shed, examined the stump of the telegraph pole and then searched the long grass that surrounded it. He took measurements and collected samples as he did so, and it took him most of the day.

The night before, Ivo had, with some difficulty, limped out to the garden and moved the Nihilator to the old outhouse, where he had hidden it with the robot under some plastic sheeting. He had thought this was enough to keep them safe but, before he left, the engineer came to the house to ask Mrs Radomir if she had kept any strange chemicals in the shed, anything that might have caught fire or exploded. When she told him the shed had mostly been used by Ivo to build a robot, he was very interested. He had done some work on robots himself, he said, and hoped Ivo would be kind enough to show it to him when he came back the following day.

Clearly the *Indestructible* and the Nihilator had to be hidden somewhere else before he returned, and the obvious place to take them was Douglas's house. Ivo could not take them there himself – with his foot in plaster and his crutches, he could barely walk the length of the garden – so Douglas would have to come and get them. If he put them in the barrow he would be able to wheel them home and hide them, either in his garage or in the annexe.

Ivo rang Douglas at four o'clock to suggest this, but there was no reply. He had rung again every ten minutes for the next hour and a half, but there was still no answer.

Whether Douglas was there or not, Ivo thought, somehow he had to get the robot round to the house in Western Avenue. He hobbled down the garden and looked at the shape hidden in the outhouse, wondering what he should do.

And then he realized the answer had been staring him in the face all along.

'Did you know,' Quomp was sitting in an armchair, pouring himself a second cup of tea, 'that the hundred years after the Touchstones were discovered are called the Years of Chaos? Anyone who got hold of one kept it and the result was a century of suffering and misery beyond belief. It was a terrible time, more terrible than you can imagine. We got control of things eventually, of course. It wasn't easy, but people came to see it was the only way forward. And we've had almost undisturbed peace for nearly ten thousand years as a result.'

Quomp paused while he added a splash of milk to his cup then drank his tea, sucking the liquid up his nose in a single breath before mopping away the drips with his handkerchief.

'The problem is, you see, that Gedrus will tell you anything. Anything at all. If you want to build a nuclear bomb or set off a plague that'll wipe out half the population of the planet, he'll tell you how to do it as happily as he'll give instructions on how to make a mug of Horlicks. Here . . .' Quomp reached into his pocket, drew out the Touchstone and threw it to Douglas. 'If you don't believe me, you can ask him yourself.'

Douglas caught the stone by its silver chain, but made no move to touch it. 'I don't want to build a nuclear bomb,' he said. 'Or start a plague. I never . . .'

'Whether you *wanted* to or not isn't important,' the Guardian interrupted. 'The point I'm making is that if you asked, Gedrus would tell you how. Because that's what he does. It doesn't matter to him if you want to murder someone or save the universe. He just tells people whatever they want to know.

'And that means he'll tell Kai whatever she wants to know as well.' Quomp carefully placed his cup and saucer back on the tray as he continued. 'He'll tell her how to raise an army and how to build the most powerful weapons in the galaxy. He'll tell her what her enemies are planning and the best way to defeat them. Now she has a Touchstone no one will be able to stand in her way, and even if the other side managed to kill her or destroy the stone, she's got a couple of spares, hasn't she? To be passed on to someone else to carry on the struggle.'

'Kai wanted to help her people,' said Douglas. He could remember the pain in the alien's eyes as she sat in the kitchen and described the suffering of her world and how she wanted to end it. 'And they needed help.

She was fighting for them because she knew it was the right thing to do.'

'Ah yes. The right thing . . .' Quomp let out a long sigh as he sat back and stared up at the ceiling. 'In my experience most of the trouble in the galaxy has been caused by people who knew they were doing the right thing.'

'She was asking Gedrus to help her overthrow a tyrant,' said Douglas. 'How could that be bad?'

'It can be bad because it was the wrong question.' Quomp took out a handkerchief and began busily polishing his glasses. 'And you can do a lot of damage if you ask Gedrus the wrong question.'

It came into Douglas's mind that he had had the same thought himself, when he found that asking Gedrus to help bring his parents back together had only made things worse for everyone around him.

'What's the right question then?' he asked.

The Guardian did not appear to hear.

'We can't let her take the Touchstones back to her homeworld.' He put his glasses back on his nose and looked across at Douglas. 'That's the number one priority. We have to stop her before she leaves this planet. And I need to know if you're going to help me.'

Douglas hesitated. 'Who says you should have a Touchstone and not Kai?'

'I should have thought that was obvious,' Quomp said, standing up, 'but it's not what we're discussing here. I need an answer. Are you going to help me or not?'

'I . . . I don't know,' said Douglas.

'Well . . .' The Guardian picked up the tea tray. 'I can give you a few minutes to make up your mind. But don't take too long.'

He began walking to the door.

'What happens if I don't help?' asked Douglas.

'If you mean will you be punished in some way,' Quomp paused in the doorway, 'the answer is no, you won't. If you don't want to help I will leave and your life will go back to the way it was. But the real answer to your question is that if you don't help, Kai will get away. She'll return to her planet, we will follow and there will be a war in which many, many thousands of people will die. You might want to bear that in mind while you're making your decision.'

And he was gone.

Douglas stared at the closing door for some seconds before he realized that he still had the Touchstone, hanging by its silver chain from his fingers.

Ivo had known, even as he steered the robot out of the outhouse, that it was not going to be an easy journey. The *Indestructible* was large enough for him to sit on, and moved very smoothly, but the force field that surrounded the robot made it feel as if he was sitting on polished glass. It was almost impossible to hold himself in place at the same time as working the remote control, and twice he slid off completely before he stopped and tied himself on with a length of washing line.

It was quite tricky even then. He really needed both hands to steer the robot with the remote control, but he also had to carry his crutches under one arm and the Nihilator under the other. Holding it tightly as he went round a corner, the bone in his elbow inadvertently pressed the trigger – and an arc of energy flashed out in front of him and a bus shelter and most of a maple tree in the garden behind it disappeared.

It meant further delay while he stopped to work out somewhere safer to keep the weapon and then he wondered if he should leave a note of apology about the bus shelter. Eventually he put the Nihilator in the hood of his anorak, decided it was safest not to write anything and continued on his way, determinedly ignoring the people that turned to stare as he sped by.

When he finally arrived at Douglas's house he noticed a maroon 4x4 Toyota parked in the driveway.

It looked as if Douglas had a visitor.

The more Douglas thought about it, the harder it was to make a decision. Kai wanted to get back to her home planet to fight for her people's freedom, which seemed perfectly reasonable. Gedrus had shown him what was being done to them by the tyrant, and there was no doubt that the sooner he was overthrown the better. With the Touchstone she could do it, and without it she would be defeated.

But according to Gedrus, Quomp had been telling the truth as well. Everything he said about the Years of Chaos and the peace that the Guardians had brought to the Federation was true. And Douglas could also see that, in the wrong hands, the Touchstones were extremely dangerous. If the Guardians were prepared to go to war to get the stolen Touchstones back from Kai, maybe he should do what Quomp said and . . .

Douglas paced restlessly up and down. It would be much easier to make a decision if he could see that one side was wrong and the other was right but, as far as he could make out, you could argue for either side. You couldn't say either of them was bad – at least Douglas couldn't – but somehow he had to choose between them. He *had* to choose. Even not choosing would be a choice because if he refused to help Quomp it would mean that Kai would get away.

It wasn't just a difficult decision, Douglas thought. It was an impossible one. He was twelve years old. He didn't know enough to make a decision like this. He didn't *begin* to know enough.

He stared at the stone, lying on the sofa where he'd left it. The one person who *did* know enough was Gedrus, because Gedrus knew everything. But if Douglas had learnt anything over the last few weeks it was that asking Gedrus for help did not necessarily make things better.

You could ask Gedrus how to build a robot and wind up putting a friend in hospital. You could ask him to help with your homework and find it led to someone else running away from home. You could ask him to help get your parents back together and find it did exactly the opposite of what you wanted.

All he wanted to do was whatever was best and yet . . .

And yet . . .

And from nowhere, he had it. If that really was all he wanted to do, then the answer was simple. So simple he couldn't think why he hadn't thought of it before. It was all a matter of asking the right question and, for the first time, he had an inkling of what the right question might be. He picked up the Touchstone.

'Hi there!' Gedrus was sitting at his desk doing a crossword puzzle. 'What can I do for you?'

'I have to choose,' said Douglas, 'whether to help Guardian Quomp get the Touchstones back from Kai, or let her get away.'

'Oh yes?'

'And I don't know enough about Guardians and Federation politics to know what to do, but you know everything about all those things, don't you? So what I want is for you to tell me the best thing to do.'

'Hmmm.' Gedrus drummed his fingers lightly on the desk. 'Would this be best for you personally? Or best for . . .'

'Just . . . best,' said Douglas, 'for everyone. I want to do whatever is going to help the most people and not hurt anybody at all, if possible. If you want me to keep quiet and help Kai, I'll do that. If you want me to help Quomp, I'll do that. And if there's another idea that's better than either of those, I'll do that instead. You're the one who knows. You tell me what to do and I'll do it.' He paused. 'You can tell me, can't you?'

'Oh yes,' Gedrus nodded. 'No problem there.'

'OK,' Douglas took a deep breath. 'So what should I do?'

And Gedrus told him.

The Guardian was standing at the sink in the kitchen. He had taken off his jacket and was wearing Mrs Paterson's apron while he washed up the tea things. He turned round when he heard Douglas come in.

'Have you decided?'

'Yes,' said Douglas. 'If there's something you want me to do, I'll do it.'

'Good.' From under his bushy eyebrows, Quomp looked carefully at Douglas as he dried his hands on a towel. 'And may I ask how you came to this decision?'

'I asked Gedrus what would be best and he told me just to do whatever you said.'

'Was that best for . . . yourself?'

'No,' said Douglas. 'Just what was best. For everybody. What would do the least harm and the most good. That sort of thing.'

For the first time since Douglas had seen him, the Guardian smiled. It was a warm and surprisingly gentle smile.

'Well, it's not the official phrasing, but close enough.' He put a hand on Douglas's shoulder. 'You had me worried for a minute. I thought you weren't going to get there. But you did. Well done!'

'I don't understand,' said Douglas.

'No,' Quomp nodded, 'and you are owed a good many explanations, but first . . .'

Before he could finish his sentence the Guardian was interrupted by the noise of the back door slamming open as Ivo, sitting on the *Indestructible*, crashed into the kitchen and spun the robot through ninety degrees to face him. In one quick movement he pulled the Nihilator from the hood of his anorak and pointed it directly at the Guardian's head.

'Take your hands off my friend,' he said in a voice that was only slightly shaking, 'or you're dead.'

The Guardian stared for a moment at the weapon, then at Ivo and then back at Douglas.

'Is that a Nihilator?' His voice rose in horror as he spoke. 'It is, isn't it! You've built a Nihilator!'

'I'm going to give you three seconds,' said Ivo. 'One . . .'

'Have you any *idea* how dangerous those things are?' Quomp's voice was full of indignation. 'For goodness sake, put it down before someone gets hurt.'

'Two,' said Ivo.

'Put it down, Ivo,' said Douglas and as his friend hesitated, he added, 'It's all right . . . I think.'

CHAPTER ELEVEN

'The thing is,' said Quomp, 'we don't have much time.'

He was standing in the dining room, stabbing deftly at a number of buttons on a small device he had placed on the centre of the table. As he did so an image of the earth appeared above it, a vivid sphere of blue and green covered in slowly moving clouds.

'Kai is somewhere on the planet,' Quomp pointed to the image, 'building a ship to take her home. We calculate she could be ready to leave any time in the coming week but we don't know where she is or how to stop her.'

Looking closer Douglas could see there were two groups of ships, like clusters of flies, orbiting the image of earth. The image flickered for a moment until Quomp thumped the device impatiently before continuing.

'We have two battle fleets patrolling each hemisphere and, once she's launched, they will be able to detect her. But Gedrus says they won't be able to destroy her before she disappears into y-space. She'll be gone before we can overpower her defence shields.'

The boys watched as a tiny gleam of light launched up from the surface of earth. The black ships moved towards it, several of them firing beams of glowing orange light, but the ship continued moving until, a few inches from Ivo's nose, it suddenly disappeared.

'If she gets home, it'll take an army to stop her. We have to find her *before* she leaves the planet.' Quomp leaned forward, turned off the device and the image disappeared. 'But she has a Touchstone so it won't be easy.'

'You found Douglas,' said Ivo.

'Douglas was obliging enough to draw attention to himself by buying shares.' The Guardian walked over to the window and briskly drew back the curtains. 'But Kai won't be so helpful. The first thing she'll have done is ask Gedrus to warn her if anything she plans to do might give her away.'

Douglas wondered why he hadn't thought of doing this himself.

'We only have one chance.' His hands behind his back, the Guardian turned to face the boys. 'And it's Douglas.'

'What can I do?' asked Douglas.

'You can send Kai a message through Gedrus, saying you want to see her before she goes.'

Douglas looked doubtful. 'You think she'd agree to that?'

'It's possible,' said Quomp. 'You saved her life so she owes you a life debt. The Vangarians take that sort of thing very seriously.'

'But won't she know it's a trap?' asked Ivo.

'How can it be a trap?' said Quomp patiently. 'She has a Touchstone. If I ordered troops to lie in wait and ambush her she'd know about the orders before the troops even boarded their transport. She'll have asked Gedrus to tell her if anyone is planning an attack.' He turned back to Douglas. 'When you meet her, you will be entirely alone. Neither I nor anyone else will be at hand. It's the only way this will work.'

'So what do I do when I see her?' asked Douglas.

The Guardian took a deep breath. 'You explain to her that taking the stones back to her people will cause more harm than good and ask her not to do it, but to return the Touchstones to me.'

There was a long pause while the boys looked at him.

'That's the plan?' said Douglas, doubtfully.

Quomp nodded.

'You want him to *persuade* her to give back the Touchstones?' said Ivo.

'Yes.'

'I don't think it'll work,' said Douglas.

'Well, if it doesn't work, it doesn't work.' The Guardian's face had taken on a defensive look. 'But it's what we have to do because Gedrus says it's the best thing.' He turned to Douglas. 'Will you do it?'

Douglas thought about it, but only for a moment. Gedrus had been very definite that he should do whatever Quomp told him and if the Guardian wanted him to talk to Kai, there was no reason he could think of to say no.

'Yes,' he said. 'Of course I will.'

The Guardian gave Douglas very precise instructions about how to send the message to Kai through Gedrus, and what it should say. Then he warned him that the reply might come at any time in the next few days – or not at all – but in the meantime he was to carry on with life as normally as possible.

'You won't see me, of course,' he explained as he led the way back to the kitchen to retrieve his jacket. 'I'll have to keep right out of the way. If Kai does decide to contact you, the last thing we want is for her to see me hovering in the background.'

'What's happened to my robot?' Ivo limped into the kitchen and looked round. 'It's gone.'

'I've had it destroyed.' The Guardian pulled on his jacket and straightened his tie. 'The Nihilator as well, I'm afraid. Call me old-fashioned, but there was something about the idea of a plasma cannon and a warship's force field in the hands of a twelve year old that was more than my nerves could take.' Determinedly ignoring the look on Ivo's face, he added, 'Don't worry about getting home. I'll give you a lift. But we'll have to hurry. Gedrus tells me Douglas's mother will be here in four and a quarter minutes.'

Outside he paused before climbing into the Toyota and turned to Douglas. 'Remember, you send the message this evening. If you're not certain about anything, do whatever Gedrus tells you. I'll be in touch when all this is over.'

Douglas nodded, and the Guardian glanced across to where Ivo had already heaved himself into the passenger seat. 'Have you two known each other long?'

'Not really,' said Douglas. 'Only a few weeks.'

'Interesting.' The Guardian paused with his hand on the door. 'Not everyone would have done what he did. Must be good to know you've got a friend like that at your back, eh?'

Douglas thought what it must have been like for Ivo to arrive at the house, look through the kitchen window, see a man with a Touchstone, realize he must be a Guardian and then burst in and point a Nihilator at his head.

'Yes,' he said. 'Yes, it is.'

When he finally got to bed that night Douglas felt it had been a very long day.

His mother had arrived home almost immediately

after Quomp had driven off, and announced that she had left her job at the supermarket. A few minutes later, sitting at the kitchen table, while Douglas got a chicken curry from the freezer and put it in the microwave for supper, she burst into tears and admitted that she had not left her job but been fired.

'I can't even manage the checkout at a supermarket,' she wailed, tears streaming down her cheeks, 'I can't do anything. I'm useless!'

It had taken nearly an hour to calm her down and then Mr Paterson rang from Germany to ask if everything was all right and the crying began all over again. Douglas found he was rather glad when it was time for bed.

He had sent the message to Kai. It was very short, simply saying that if it was possible, he would like to see her again before she left. Gedrus assured him it had been delivered but was not allowed to say whether Kai had read it or not.

Although it had been a long day, there was one more thing Douglas had to do before he went to sleep. Lying on his bed, he reached for the Touchstone again and found the librarian at his desk watching television.

'Hi there!' Gedrus turned off the sound and swung round to face Douglas. 'What can I do for you?'

'I'd like to do something for my parents,' said Douglas. 'And something for Ivo and Hannah as well. To make up for what I did before.'

'OK.' Gedrus picked up a notebook and pen. 'What did you have in mind?'

'Well, I thought it might be better if you worked that out,' said Douglas. 'I'd just like to do whatever is best. I mean, if you think it's best that I don't do anything then I won't, but if there was anything I could do that would help any of them, I'd like to do it.'

'Right.' Gedrus leaned back in his chair. 'Well, I could make some suggestions.'

'Thank you,' said Douglas and he listened carefully while Gedrus outlined what he had in mind.

It looked as if tomorrow was going to be a long day as well.

The next day was Saturday and, after breakfast, Douglas told his mother he was cycling round to see Ivo. It was true that he was planning to call in on his friend but in fact he cycled first to Mr Linneker's house.

The headmaster lived in a large Victorian villa on the south side of the town and, when he answered the door, Douglas hardly recognized him. He hadn't shaved, his shirt was hanging out of his trousers, there were dark rings under his eyes and he looked as if he hadn't slept for days.

'This isn't a good time, Douglas,' he muttered. 'Why don't you come to my office on Monday?'

'It's about Hannah,' said Douglas. 'I know where she is.'

The headmaster stared at him, blankly.

'She's gone to Norwich. Where you used to live.' Douglas took a piece of paper from his pocket. 'She's got several friends there but she's staying with this one.'

Mr Linneker took the paper and stared at it.

'Her name's Laura. She was her best friend and she's letting Hannah stay in the attic. She hides in the wardrobe if anyone comes up.'

Mr Linneker was still staring at the name and address in his hand.

'The thing is,' Douglas went on, 'it's partly my fault that she ran away and I . . .'

But the headmaster was no longer listening. 'Margaret!' he shouted indoors, 'Margaret! I've found out where she's gone!'

Douglas waited on the doorstep for a moment. There was a lot more he had been planning to say, but the noise from inside the house seemed to suggest that now was not the time. He could hear the headmaster shouting for his shoes, the car keys, his mobile phone . . . and Douglas walked back to his bicycle.

He was at the corner when the headmaster's car raced past him, with Mr Linneker at the wheel. He was heading for Norwich like a bat out of hell and didn't notice Douglas at all.

Douglas's second visit was to Mr Parrot, who welcomed him into his tiny office with his usual beaming smile, and a box of doughnuts.

'I was hoping you'd call in today.' He took a dough-nut for himself and pushed the box towards Douglas. 'I wanted to check that everything was all right.'

'I think so,' said Douglas. 'Why?'

'Well . . .' Mr Parrot leaned forward and spoke in a confidential whisper, 'I was thinking about that burglary yesterday and it's just possible that what they were after was your name and address. People know that I'm getting information from somewhere and I was worried someone might be planning to ask you to tell them what shares to buy. Has . . . anything like that happened?'

'No,' said Douglas. 'Nothing like that.'

'Well, let me know if it does. Can't have you bothered by that sort of thing.' The financial adviser leaned back into his chair. 'Now, what can I do for you?'

'Two things,' said Douglas. 'One, I'd like to buy a shed for my friend, Ivo. He had this workshop in his garden that got knocked down, and it was partly my fault so I'd like to replace it. But I'd like to do it anonymously. Could you organize that?'

'How about I tell him it's a gift from a local philan-thropist? Someone who read about the accident in the paper and felt sorry for him,' said Mr Parrot. 'It does happen occasionally.' Then he listened as Douglas explained how big the shed should be and what it would need in the way of tools and workbenches, carefully writing it all down in his notebook.

'The other thing I'd like to do is lend my father

sixty thousand pounds. He's invented this super-market trolley that always steers in the right direction but he needs some money to develop it.'

'Sixty thousand pounds to your father . . .' Mr Parrot carefully noted down the figure, wondering if any other financial advisors took instructions like this from their twelve-year-old clients. 'You think it'll be a winner, do you? This trolley?'

'It's probably going to make him very rich,' said Douglas, 'but I'd prefer him not to know the money came from me. Not yet anyway. Is that all right?'

'Your father told me I was to let you invest your money wherever you wanted,' said Mr Parrot, hap-pily. 'I'm sure we can keep the secret a little longer.' He opened a drawer in his desk. 'I'll need you to sign a few forms and, while you're doing that, you can tell me if you've seen any more of your pictures.'

'Pictures?'

'The pictures you get that tell you what shares to buy,' Mr Parrot explained.

It might be his last chance, Douglas thought, and he reached into his pocket for the Touchstone.

Gedrus told him that shares in a company called Plasco, which made optical data storage systems, were likely to do very well in the coming week, and Mr Parrot was delighted at the news.

Douglas's third visit was to a large modern building in a road off the High Street, called the Greenwood

Dance Studio. Inside, the entrance hall was painted entirely in shades of green and filled with green furniture. The young man behind the reception desk was dressed in a green silk shirt, had green highlights in his hair and was talking on the phone in loud, urgent tones.

'You can't do this to me!' he was saying. 'I've got nearly two hundred pupils. Who's going to look after them?' He lowered his voice as the door opened and Douglas came in. 'Look, if it's the money, I'm sure we can work something out, but you have to . . .'

But whoever he was talking to had hung up and he slowly replaced the phone. 'What do you want?' he asked Douglas, without looking up.

'Do you teach ballroom dancing here?'

'We used to,' muttered the man, 'until about three minutes ago.'

'I was thinking of learning myself.' Douglas seemed quite unperturbed by the man's lack of interest. 'My mother did a lot of ballroom dancing. She was Home Counties Latin American Champion three years in a row.'

'Your mother?' A flicker of interest crossed the man's face and he looked up. 'What was her name?'

'Rachel,' said Douglas. 'Rachel Paterson. Well, she was Rachel Findlay then of course. It was before she was married.'

'Rachel Findlay?' The man's eyes widened. 'Your mother is Rachel Findlay?'

'You've heard of her?'

'Well, of course I've heard of her!' The man at the desk came round to stand beside Douglas, who noticed he was wearing green trousers and green suede shoes as well. 'I saw her win the Hesketh trophy in 1991. She taught me to salsa.'

'Really?'

'Not that she'd remember – I was only thirteen – she was giving lessons to anyone who . . .' The man stopped, struck by a sudden thought. 'She wouldn't be interested in a job, would she?'

'What sort of job?'

'Teaching! Teaching dance!' The man banged his fist on the reception desk in his enthusiasm. 'I mean, if there was any chance she was free . . . any chance at all . . .'

'Well,' said Douglas thoughtfully, 'I'll give you our phone number. It might be worth giving her a call.'

It was nearly midday before Douglas finally arrived at Ivo's house in Raglan Road and the first thing Ivo wanted to know was whether he had heard anything from Kai.

'No,' Douglas told him. 'Not yet.' He had checked with Gedrus several times in the course of the morning but the answer had always been the same.

'You're quite sure it's all right, are you?' said Ivo. 'Doing what Quomp tells you to do?'

'It's what Gedrus said was best,' said Douglas. 'He was very definite.'

'But what if he's wrong?'

'I don't think Gedrus can be wrong.' Douglas frowned. 'That's not how it works.'

He was feeling rather gloomy as he walked down the garden, with Ivo swinging expertly on his crutches, to see the remains of the shattered shed. The truth was that the events of the last two days were beginning to tell, even on someone as naturally calm as Douglas, and he was not finding it easy. He had started biting his nails, something he had never done in his life, and found it difficult to think about anything except the coming meeting with Kai – and yet the more he thought about it the more unsettled he became.

In his mind, he was constantly going over all the things he might say to Kai when he saw her, all the words he might use to persuade her to return what she had stolen to Quomp. But the more he thought about it, the more it seemed that persuading Kai to surrender the Touchstones was a very forlorn hope and, what was worse, Gedrus seemed to agree with him. He had asked the librarian what his chances of success were and the reply had not been encouraging.

'Slim,' Gedrus had said as cheerfully as ever. 'Very slim.'

Douglas and Ivo spent the afternoon working on the plans for a new robot, one that would not attract quite as much attention as the *Indestructible*, but might still have a chance of winning the *Robot Wars*. It kept Douglas busy at least, and stopped him thinking too much about why there had been no answer from Kai.

It also meant, as he sat hunched over the plans, that he did not notice Ivo quietly slipping two tiny balls, each no bigger than a BB gun pellet, one into the pocket of his coat and another into the back of his school bag.

But then Ivo was very careful to do it while Douglas was looking the other way.

When Mrs Radomir told Douglas it was time to go home, there was still no word from Kai. There was still nothing when he went to bed that night, and nothing the next morning. When it finally happened it was almost a relief.

Douglas was walking back from Ivo's house the following afternoon when a car drew up alongside the pavement and the driver, whose face was largely hidden under dark glasses and a brightly coloured scarf, rolled down the window and called to him.

'Greetings, Douglas Paterson,' said Kai. She gestured to the seat beside her. 'You wanted to see me?'

'Yes, I did,' said Douglas as he climbed into the car. 'Very much. How are you?'

'All the better for seeing you, my friend.' Kai smiled and held out a hand.

As soon as Douglas touched it a light glowed from

her fingers, a warm tingling spread rapidly up his arm, there was a faint roaring sound in his ears, like waves crashing on a distant shoreline . . .

And that was the last thing he remembered.

CHAPTER TWELVE

Douglas had no idea where they were.

When he woke up he was still sitting in the car, but it was parked at the end of a long dirt track surrounded by a dense mass of trees. Directly ahead of him was a large building of rusting, corrugated iron that might once have been a barn or a small aircraft hangar.

Kai was holding open the door. 'Come,' she smiled down at him. 'This way.'

She led him across the track to the building and when Douglas followed her inside he found himself in a huge open space with no windows, but lit with a dazzling brilliance by a series of lights hung round the top of the walls.

The cement floor was almost entirely covered by an extraordinary variety of equipment. There were workbenches stacked with computer screens, banks of electronic equipment and rows of chemicals in glass jars. In one corner to his right there was a small forge, to the left was a pile of gas cylinders and a welding torch. Scattered over any spare sections of floor were metal sheets, steel rods, iron plates and wire coils, while at the far end, looking a little out of place, Douglas could see a large pink double bed and a kitchen area with a cooker and fridge alongside it. But none of these things were what caught his eye as soon as he stepped inside the door.

What caught his eye, standing on the floor in the centre of the barn, was a Harrier jump jet. Douglas knew it was a Harrier because he had once made a model of it from a plastic kit, and this one even had the RAF roundels still visible on its wings.

The plane was attached by dozens of cables and hoses to a variety of boxes, tanks and cylinders so that it looked like an animal that had been chained up to keep it on the ground. It made noises like an animal too. There was a constant humming sound, with the odd bark of an electrical flash and the occasional hiss and puff of escaping gas. It gave Douglas the impression, somehow, of enormous power that could barely be contained and was eager to be unleashed.

He stared at it, open-mouthed.

'That,' said Kai, 'is what will take me home.'

'You can fly a Harrier jump jet into space?' said Douglas. 'Are you sure?'

'It was a useful framework.' Kai led the way to an

aluminium ladder that led up to a section of staging alongside the plane. 'But it is not the metal that will protect me. The plane is surrounded by a force field, devised by the Tenebrians. Here, let me show you.'

Douglas followed her up the ladder and found himself looking down into the cockpit where Kai pointed to a tightly wound mass of copper wire very similar to the shape he and Ivo had made for the *Indestructible*, though much larger. The control panel was laid out with rows of switches, dials and gauges, mostly held in place by large quantities of sticky tape and, instead of a joystick, there was what looked like the steering wheel from a car.

'This can fly you back to your homeworld?' asked Douglas.

'It will fly me to a portal,' said Kai. 'Going through the portal will bring me to a few light years from my home planet where . . . arrangements have been made to get me home.'

'Are you leaving soon?'

'In a few hours.' Kai gestured to the equipment that surrounded her. 'The shields need another hour to reach full charge and there is some weaponry to load but . . . I shall be ready before evening.'

Douglas stared at the plane and then at all the equipment that surrounded it. 'You built all this in three weeks?'

Kai gave a little shrug. 'I had Gedrus to guide me.

You have probably discovered for yourself what can be achieved with his help.'

'Yes. Yes, I have.'

'And I would like to hear of your adventures.' Kai was climbing back down the ladder. 'Come, we shall sit down and you shall tell me your story.'

Ivo was already waiting on the pavement when the maroon 4x4 Toyota drew up in front of the house in Raglan Road. He hopped straight over to it, pulled open the door and swung himself up into the passenger seat.

'I still think this is most unwise,' said Guardian Quomp from the driving seat. 'It could be dangerous, and there's no point. No point at all.'

'Sorry,' Ivo was already fastening his seat belt, 'but I'm coming. You promised, remember?'

'That doesn't mean it's a good idea.' Quomp looked unhappily over the top of his glasses. 'What did you tell your parents?'

'I told them a friend of Douglas was taking us out somewhere and that we'd be back later this afternoon.'

Quomp grunted, hesitated a moment longer, then reached forward to switch on the ignition.

'Well, if you insist on coming you can at least make yourself useful. Here.' He passed Ivo a grey metal object about the size of a thin paperback book. 'You can navigate.'

★

'So tell me,' Kai said, leading Douglas across the barn to a battered wooden table and two plastic upright chairs, 'what uses did you find for your Touchstone?'

'A lot of things really,' said Douglas. 'I tried to get my parents back together.'

'You used it to restore family unity?' Kai nodded, approvingly. 'A noble purpose.'

'Unfortunately it didn't work out quite like I expected. I had to stop when I found out it was only making them unhappy.'

'I am sorry to hear that,' said Kai gravely.

'A lot of the things I asked Gedrus to do turned out like that,' Douglas went on. 'I helped Ivo build a robot and he ended up in hospital with a broken foot. And I helped this girl in my class with some homework and it led to her running away from home.'

'The Touchstone is a powerful force,' said Kai thoughtfully. 'Perhaps I was wrong to let you keep it.'

'No, no, I'm glad you did,' Douglas insisted, 'only it made me realize you have to be really careful what you ask. You have to know exactly what you want and then phrase it very carefully, don't you? Which is why I'm here in a way.'

He hesitated.

'Yes?' said Kai.

'Well, the thing is, I've come to ask you to do something.'

'I suspected as much when you sent me the message.' Kai smiled as she settled herself into a chair.

'Fear not, Douglas! I owe you a life debt. If your request is within my power, you have my word that I shall not hesitate to grant it. What is it you want me to do?'

The flat screen that Quomp had given Ivo showed a picture of the road ahead with a dotted green line indicating the route they should take and even warning of hazards like roadworks or traffic jams. It was a lot easier to use than a map and they were making good progress until, after about an hour, they came to a small village. They had slowed to turn right up a hill when a car shot out of the drive on their left and crashed straight into the side of the Toyota.

The car was an elderly Volvo that looked as if it had been involved in several accidents before. Inside, with only her eyes and the top of her head visible above the steering wheel, was an elderly, white-haired lady.

'I'm so sorry,' she said when Quomp came round to see if she was all right. 'I was trying to reverse into the garage. I must have got the wrong gear.'

'Are you hurt?' asked the Guardian.

'No, no, I'm fine.' The old lady was fumbling in the glove compartment of the car. 'I've got my insurance certificate in here somewhere . . .'

'Please don't worry about it,' said Quomp. 'As long as no one was hurt, I suggest we forget about it and . . .'

'But your car!'

'It's nothing.' Quomp glanced at the crumpled side doors of his own vehicle and waved a hand dismissively. 'A mere scratch.'

'It looks like more than a scratch to me.' A policeman had appeared and was staring at the damage, shaking his head. 'What happened?'

'It's nothing,' said Quomp. 'We've already agreed to . . .'

The policeman held up his hand. 'One thing at a time, sir. One thing at a time.' He turned to the old lady. 'What did you do this time, Doris?'

'Is this going to take very long?' asked Ivo when the Guardian came back to the car.

'Gedrus tells me it may take some minutes to sort out.' Quomp was holding the Touchstone in his fingers and looking anxiously at his watch. 'But unfortunately, he also believes we have very few minutes to spare.'

Douglas had spent most of the last two days working out what he should say when this moment came but now it had arrived it still wasn't easy to find the right words.

Kai was looking at him expectantly.

'Well,' he said eventually, 'you know when I found you in the garden, you told me you had to take the Touchstones back to your planet so you could win the war you were fighting and free your people?'

133

'Of course,' said Kai. 'You earned the gratitude of myself and all my people that day.'

'Right,' said Douglas, 'and when you get home you're going to ask Gedrus how you can win the war and overthrow the tyrant.'

Kai nodded. 'Preparations have already begun. My plans are laid.'

'Yes,' Douglas hesitated. 'Well, I wondered if that was what you really wanted.'

Kai smiled. 'I can promise you, I have wanted nothing else since I was a child.'

'Isn't what you really want,' said Douglas, 'just to do whatever is best for your people?'

Kai frowned. 'The best thing for my people would be the overthrow of the tyrant that enslaves, tortures and imprisons them, and has robbed them of their freedom.' The smile had faded from her lips and, with her right hand, she was lightly fingering the Touchstone round her neck. 'What exactly is your request, Douglas?'

'You could be right, about winning the war being the best thing for your planet, but . . .' Something in the way Kai looked at him was making Douglas distinctly nervous, 'but I wondered if it was worth checking, you know? With Gedrus?'

Kai was very still now. Not even her fingers moved as she held the stone around her neck.

'That's my request,' said Douglas. 'That's why I came here. I'd just like you to ask Gedrus what's the best thing to do with the stones you took. What's the best thing for your people.'

Kai still did not move or speak but her eyes bored into Douglas, every muscle in her body was tense and suddenly –

'You've been caught!' She spat out the words as she sprang to her feet. 'The Guardians found you and sent you here, didn't they!' Reaching across the table, she grabbed Douglas by the front of his shirt and hauled him to his feet. 'They told you to come here, didn't they?' Her grip tightened. 'Answer me!'

Douglas managed to nod his head.

'Who? Who found you?'

'He's called Quomp. He's the Guardian for the Seventeenth Quadrant.'

'Aaarrrgh!' With a great roar Kai threw him to one side so that his head and arm banged sharply against the wall and he fell to the floor, stunned, and with an excruciating pain in his shoulder.

Kai was striding across the room to the ship, shouting as she went, 'A trap! A trap! And I walked into it like a three-week-old cub!'

As she spoke she was stabbing rapidly at the buttons and switches on a control panel beneath the ship and, a moment later, a deep humming of energy pulsed through the floors and ceiling with a power that literally made Douglas's hair stand on end. The lights dimmed and, in the centre of the floor, the Harrier began to glow, the dull green of its paintwork

135

covered in a flickering, luminescent blue.

'No!' Douglas was struggling to his feet, despite the pain in his head and arm. 'You don't understand.'

Kai had left the control panel and was striding across to one of the workbenches, which she threw to one side as if it had been made of paper, and knelt on the floor.

'I trusted you, Douglas Paterson!' She spun round and pointed a finger at him. 'And you have betrayed me to my enemies.'

Kneeling on the ground, she lifted a steel trapdoor and reached down into a hole in the floor.

'Please!' Douglas walked towards her, clutching his elbow. 'I haven't betrayed anyone. It's only me. It's not a trap. There's nobody else, I promise.'

'If you believe that, you're an even bigger fool than I am.' Kai pulled out the case that Douglas immediately recognized as the one containing the two remaining Touchstones. 'They have used you to find me. And I let them.'

'The Guardian wanted me to make you ask the question,' said Douglas. 'That's all. That's the only reason I'm here. You have to ask Gedrus if what you are doing will help your people.'

'You think I need to ask a librarian if fighting for freedom is the right thing to do?' With the case under one arm, Kai was striding back towards the ship, picking up a helmet and a jumpsuit on the way. 'You think I would let someone else decide if my people should be allowed to suffer or for how long?'

'But you have to ask him,' Douglas pleaded. 'That's what Gedrus is for! Maybe he'll say it's all right. Maybe he'll say there's something better you could do, but you have to ask him. You promised!'

'I promised to pay a life debt to you, Douglas.' Kai was standing beneath the Harrier, pulling on the jumpsuit over her other clothes. 'Not to the puppet master who told you to contact me because it was the only way to track me down.'

'But he didn't!' said Douglas. 'I'm not here because the Guardian told me to come. I'm here because Gedrus said it was the best thing to do.'

Kai had pulled the suit up over her arms and was strapping a weapons belt round her waist.

'And did Gedrus also tell you that choosing to do the best thing might be dangerous?'

She came striding over to Douglas, to stand directly in front of him. He never saw the weapon in her hand, but the beam of light that came from it slammed into his chest with the force of a steam train and sent him fifteen metres backwards to land with a bone-breaking crash against the wall behind.

Oddly, as he slid down to the ground, the one thought that came into his mind was that being shot must have done something funny to his eyes. As he stared at the wall opposite, parts of it seemed to be bulging inwards. Like paint under the heat of a flame, sections of the corrugated iron were blistering up in great bubbles. At the same time the air filled with an acrid smell and energy crackled visibly round the room in blue and yellow sparks that danced from workbench to workbench.

A second later one of the bubbles burst and, at head height, a swarm of metal objects the size of tennis balls flew into the room spitting flashes of light. Kai, standing on the ladder, poised to climb into the Harrier, used the weapon in her hand to shoot back at them, hitting the first six, one after the other with impossible speed and accuracy.

Douglas watched as the balls tumbled to the ground but already more of them were pouring in through the hole in the wall. One of them landed on the front of the Harrier and, a moment later, both it and most of the nosecone disappeared in a blaze of light. Kai, meanwhile, had shot down a dozen more but then one settled on the back of her neck, buzzing like an angry bee. She raised a hand to pull it away but before she could reach it, a glazed look came over her eyes, her hand fell and she pitched backwards off the ladder and fell crashing to the ground.

She did not move.

Above her more of the flying balls swarmed around the room, finally taking up their station in a great circle round the walls – and there was silence.

Douglas was finding it difficult to concentrate. His vision was blurring and the pain in his chest made it almost impossible to breathe, but he saw the shape that emerged through the hole in the wall. It was a squat, broad figure, encased in black metal, and it lumbered its way across the floor with a gentle whirring noise, straight over to where Douglas lay.

The pain in his chest was getting worse as the figure halted by his feet, raised its arms and pulled off its helmet to reveal the round and slightly sweaty face of Guardian Quomp. The Guardian knelt down and put a hand behind Douglas's head. Douglas found to his relief that the pain disappeared almost at once.

'I'm sorry,' he said. 'I tried to persuade her . . .'

'It doesn't matter,' said Quomp.

'I tried everything but she wouldn't listen . . .'

'Don't talk. Just rest.' The Guardian smiled reassuringly and then, amazingly, there was Ivo, white-faced, peering over his shoulder.

'It's OK, Doug. You're going to be fine.' Ivo turned to the Guardian. 'He is going to be all right, isn't he?'

Quomp did not answer. He was busy strapping something to Douglas's arm. Douglas's eyes closed as he worked.

'I tried to tell her . . .' His voice was barely audible. 'But she wouldn't listen. I'm sorry . . . so sorry . . .' His head lolled to the side and a moment later he stopped breathing.

'He's dead!' Ivo's voice was shrill and panicky in the silence. 'We should have got here earlier! He's dead!'

'I know he's dead!' Quomp reached forward to tear open Douglas's shirt and a jet of blood shot up in the air. 'Now if you could please step out of the way, I have a great deal to do.'

CHAPTER THIRTEEN

'Lightning?' said Mr Paterson. '*Lightning?*'

Mrs Paterson nodded. 'Ivo saw it happen. There was a thunderstorm in the afternoon, Douglas was walking down the road and the lightning hit him in the chest.'

'There was this sort of flash,' said Ivo, 'and there he was, flat out on the ground.'

The three of them were standing in the waiting area of the County Accident and Emergency Unit. Mr Paterson had got the phone call when his plane landed at Luton, and had driven straight to the hospital where he found Mrs Paterson and Ivo already waiting.

'Is he all right?' Mr Paterson looked rather shaken. 'Is he badly hurt?'

'He was very lucky,' said Mrs Paterson. 'Ivo called for help and that man was passing.' She pointed across the waiting room to where Quomp was trying to get a cup of tea from the drinks machine. 'He turned out to be a doctor.'

'He got Douglas breathing again,' Ivo explained, 'and then brought us both to the hospital.'

When the Guardian came over to join them, Mr Paterson took his hand and shook it.

'Ivo tells me you saved our son's life.' He pumped the hand vigorously up and down. 'I don't know how to thank you.'

'I'm only glad I was there in time to help.' Quomp retrieved his hand and dabbed with a tissue at the tea that had spilled on his sleeve. 'It was a nasty accident.'

'He's going to be all right, isn't he?' asked Mrs Paterson anxiously. 'He's not in any danger?'

'I don't think there'll be any lasting effects, but of course it's not really me you want to ask.' The Guardian pointed to a man in a white coat who had come into the waiting room. 'That's the hospital doctor over there.'

As Mr and Mrs Paterson hurried away to hear the latest news from the doctor, Ivo turned to the Guardian.

'He *is* going to be all right, isn't he?' he asked.

'Unconscious for about eight hours,' said Quomp, 'physically a bit shaky for a couple of weeks but after that, absolutely fine. Could you give him a message for me, when he wakes up?'

'Sure,' said Ivo. 'What is it?'

'It's three things really. First, if you could ask him not to contradict the lightning story. It would save everyone a great deal of trouble if he didn't say anything about aliens and spaceships and being killed. I know he's not good at telling lies but perhaps he could say he doesn't remember too clearly how he was injured? I doubt they'll question him very closely, and you can always fill in the blanks. You don't mind telling untruths yourself, do you?'

'No,' said Ivo. 'It's never been a problem.'

'Good!' The Guardian took a quick look round to check no one was watching, stuck his nose in the tea and determinedly sucked it up in one long, gurgling breath. 'Second, if you could tell him I'm sorry not to be here when he wakes up, but that I'll be back in a couple of weeks and we'll sort out any problems then.'

'You're not staying?' asked Ivo.

'I wish I could,' Quomp put down his cup, 'but I have to get Kai into custody, return the Touchstones to a Federation safepoint, write my report, then sort out a crisis on Trition V . . .' He sighed. 'It's always the same story. Too many problems, not enough Guardians.' He looked over at Mr and Mrs Paterson. 'I'd better be going before someone asks for my name and address. Look after Douglas for me and I'll see you in a week or two.'

'Um, you said there were three things to tell him,' said Ivo, 'and you've only told me two.'

'Oh yes.' The Guardian paused in the doorway and

smiled. 'Tell him he did well. Tell him he did very well indeed.'

Ivo went round to see Douglas straight after school the following day. His foot was still in plaster but Mrs Paterson picked him up at the school gates and drove him to the hospital.

'He woke up some time in the early hours,' she said, 'and he's been asking to see you all day.'

She took him to the ward where Douglas was lying in a bed in the corner, with a tube running out of his arm to a plastic bottle hanging on a pole. Then she went off to get the latest report on his progress from the staff nurse.

'How are you feeling?' asked Ivo.

Mostly Douglas was feeling very confused. The last thing he remembered was lying on the floor of the barn while Quomp told him not to talk and now he was in a hospital bed with everyone telling him he'd been struck by lightning.

When they asked him what he remembered, he wasn't sure what he should say. He wasn't sure of a good many things, and his first instinct had been to reach for the Touchstone round his neck and ask Gedrus for advice. But the Touchstone wasn't there. He had asked his mother to check the pockets of his trousers but it wasn't there either. It wasn't anywhere, and a part of him had always known that it wouldn't be. Only Guardians were allowed to have

Touchstones. Quomp had been very definite about that.

'The lightning,' said Ivo, 'is a story Gedrus made up. It explains why there's a scar on your chest, and you're a bit weak and so on. I told them you were walking back from being at my house when you were hit, and all you have to say is that you can't really remember anything.'

'Oh,' said Douglas. 'And what really happened?'

'Well . . .' Ivo took a deep breath. 'What really happened was that you were dead – not for very long, fortunately, because Quomp put you back together – and then he brought you here to the hospital and I rang your house.'

'But how did you find me?'

'What?'

'How did you know where I was?'

'Ah!' Ivo nodded. 'That was the pellets. I planted these pellets in your clothes – one in your coat, one in your bag, a few more in other places later on. They were made of this metal that doesn't exist anywhere else so we could follow you with a detector. Quomp asked me to do it that evening when he took me home but I said only if he'd let me come with him.' He paused, then added, 'It was all right for me to do that, wasn't it? Only you did say doing whatever Quomp said was the best thing, didn't you?'

'Yes, I did.' Douglas stared at the ceiling. 'What happened next?'

'Well, when Kai picked you up we followed you in the car. I thought we'd be following you in some sort of spaceship but Quomp said if we used a ship it would show up on the Federation search screens and then Kai would find out about us from Gedrus. Anyway, the car was quite fast enough, or it would have been but then this old lady backed out of her drive and it was ten minutes before we could get away and even when we got to the barn, it was very difficult to get in. Quomp had about a hundred buzzbots – that's these little robots,' Ivo cupped his hands as if holding a tennis ball, 'about this big, that fly around and do anything you want, really amazing – but Kai had set up all these defence mechanisms he wasn't expecting and, even when he did get in, it was ages before the buzzbots knocked everything out. Quomp said it lasted longer than any other firefight he could remember. About five and a half seconds.'

There were sections of this story that Douglas did not entirely understand, and even larger sections that he did not understand at all, but one thing at least had become clear.

'So Kai was right? It was all a trap?'

'Oh yes.' Ivo nodded firmly. 'It was always a trap. I mean, it would have been nice if you'd persuaded Kai to give up the Touchstones on her own but Quomp said the chances of that were very slim so it seemed like he should bring along the buzzbots in case.'

'You both knew it was a trap? And you didn't tell me?'

'Gedrus told us not to,' said Ivo apologetically. 'He said if we did the whole thing might not work.' He looked down at his friend. 'Quomp says Kai didn't mean to kill you. Well, he doesn't think she did. She meant to stun you but she forgot you were only twelve years old and a human.' He peered anxiously down. 'You're looking all pale again. Are you feeling all right?'

Douglas said that he would like a glass of water and, as Ivo hobbled off to get it, he lay back on his pillow, staring into the distance. One hand reached automatically for the stone round his neck before he remembered that the Touchstone was no longer there.

He wanted to ask Gedrus to show him what had happened, to find out what had been done with Kai and her ship, to send a message to the Guardian, to ask any of the thousand questions that bubbled in his mind . . . but he couldn't. He would never be able to ask the librarian anything, ever again.

Douglas found he did not really mind about not being told about the trap. He didn't mind about being in hospital. He didn't even mind about being killed by Kai. But not to have the Touchstone round his neck was as if some vital part of himself had been amputated. He wanted, more than he could ever have imagined, to have it back. He wanted it with an intensity that was almost a physical pain and, lying there in the hospital bed, to his astonishment he found a tear trickling down his cheek.

CHAPTER FOURTEEN

Douglas was in hospital for three days. He was finally sent home on the Wednesday but, even then, the doctors said he probably should not go back to school for at least another two weeks.

Mrs Paterson had recently started her new job as dance instructor at the Greenway Studio, so there was a problem about who should look after Douglas while he was at home. There was talk about hiring a nurse but, in the end, he stayed there on his own with the phone by his bed and strict instructions to call Mrs Dewer next door if there was an emergency.

Mrs Paterson was not entirely happy with the arrangement but she could see no other choice. At the dance school she had small children about to take their first grade exams, older students preparing for national competitions and a large group of old-timers for whom the regular weekly dance session was their only social outlet. They all depended on her. She couldn't let them down.

And besides, she was thoroughly enjoying the classes. Hugely enjoying them. It was more fun than she could have believed to be back in the world of *chassés*, promenades and reverse corner turns. It was just unfortunate that Douglas should be recovering from a lightning bolt at a time when Mr Paterson was so ferociously busy with launching his supermarket trolley, and neither of them could afford to take time off work.

Douglas assured her that he didn't mind being on his own, and he meant it. He slept a good deal of the time, particularly in the first week, and when he was awake he had plenty of visitors. Ivo called in regularly. On Thursday and Friday he came round after school, and after that it was half-term and he usually hopped round on his crutches some time in the morning and again in the afternoon. He would probably have stayed all day, except that his new workshop was being built and he needed to be at home to make sure it was done properly. And once it was finished he was at work a lot of the time on the new robot.

Mr Parrot was another regular visitor. He sent a card and a vast bowl of fruit wrapped in cellophane while Douglas was in hospital, and then called in at the house in Western Avenue when Douglas came home. He brought with him an expensive-looking

MP3 player as a get-well present and a copy of his new business brochure with colour pictures of his new, very luxurious office.

'It's not too far from school,' he said cheerily, 'so you can still call in on your way home if you want to tell me about any "pictures" you've seen and what shares we ought to buy.'

Douglas told him rather sadly that he didn't think there would be any more pictures.

'Now, now.' Mr Parrot refused to be downhearted. 'None of us knows what the future holds. Give it time, eh? Give it time.'

He called round again the next week with his monthly report, which was a carefully printed sheet inside a shiny folder that said how much money Douglas had made over the last four weeks. It was an enormous sum and he asked if Douglas had any instructions as to what he should do with it.

'Not really,' said Douglas. 'Not at the moment. Could you look after it for me?'

Mr Parrot said he would be delighted. He might not be as spectacularly successful as Douglas had been, he said, but looking after people's money and making it grow was not only his job, it was what he enjoyed doing. It was what he had always wanted to do, ever since he was Douglas's age.

Another regular visitor, if an unexpected one, was Mr Linneker. The headmaster came to see Douglas while he was in hospital and then called in almost every day while he was at home. Each time he brought with him a magazine or a book he thought Douglas might enjoy and, if Douglas wasn't too tired, he would stay for a game of cards or to help with a puzzle or simply to sit and talk.

They talked a good deal, more and more as the days passed and Douglas grew stronger, and he found he looked forward to the headmaster's visits. Mr Linneker was a good talker and a keen listener and the conversation would roam over all sorts of topics – though for some reason the one thing they never talked about was Hannah. Mr Linneker never mentioned the fact that Douglas had told him where to find his daughter in Norwich, and Douglas somehow felt it would be wrong to ask what had happened.

One of the things they did talk about was Douglas's parents getting a divorce. It turned out that Mr Linneker's parents had separated when he was Douglas's age so he had been through much the same experience and knew how it felt. They had several conversations on the subject but there was one in particular that Douglas remembered.

They had been discussing why people got divorced and whose fault it might be and Mr Linneker said he was more and more convinced that, with his parents at least, it was impossible to say it had been anyone's fault.

'Looking back,' he said, 'I can see now they just

needed to go in different directions. There was no point in them staying together when they didn't want to.'

'But why didn't they want to?' asked Douglas.

'I'm not sure any of us *chooses* what we want in life,' said Mr Linneker thoughtfully. 'It's more something we discover about ourselves. I sometimes think we're all born with this sort of compass needle in our heads, telling us where we should be heading. North may be different for all of us – it makes some of us want to be engineers, others want to be businessmen, or musicians, or dancers . . . some of us even want to be teachers   it all depends which way the needle is pointing.

'And I think with my parents, and maybe with yours, that the needles were just pointing in different directions. So that's where they had to go. It doesn't mean either of them was right or wrong.'

Douglas thought about it a lot after the headmaster had gone. If there was one thing he had learnt from Gedrus it was how important it was to know exactly what you wanted, what you *really* wanted, from the deepest part of you. He thought about how some of the people around him had always seemed to know what they wanted, like Ivo or Mr Parrot. About how unhappy people could be when they didn't know what they wanted, like his mother until she got the job at the dance school. And he thought about how angry people could be if they weren't allowed to go in the direction they wanted, like Hannah wanting to be with her friends . . .

But mostly he thought about knowing exactly what it was that he wanted for himself, and how frustrating it was to realize that he could never have it. Having the Touchstone had always been more than fun or excitement or adventure. From the moment he first held it he had felt it was somehow *supposed* to be his. Knowing that he could never have it back had not altered this feeling. It simply left him with a deep and sometimes overwhelming sadness.

It was the Monday after half-term, almost two weeks after Kai had taken him out to the barn, that Douglas's most surprising visitor turned up.

Mrs Paterson had come home to make Douglas his tea, and was just getting ready to return to the dance studio when the front door bell rang.

Hannah was standing on the step. She was wearing a black skirt and black T-shirt as before, but with bright yellow tights and a yellow ribbon in her hair that made her look a bit like a wasp.

'I've come to see Douglas,' she said.

'What a splendid idea.' Mrs Paterson held open the door to let Hannah in. 'He could do with a bit of company.' She led the way across the hall to the kitchen. 'He gets left on his own a lot these days, I'm afraid, with me out at work so much of the time.' Crossing the kitchen, she held open the back door and ushered Hannah out into the garden. 'And it's not good for him. He's been getting all moody and feeling sorry for himself.'

She pointed to a figure lying on the grass at the far end of the garden. 'I keep telling him he ought to take up ballroom dancing. It's such a wonderful thing to shake you out of a depression. Have you ever tried it?'

Hannah said she didn't think ballroom dancing was really her thing.

'Well, if you ever want to give it a try, let me know.' Mrs Paterson produced a card from her pocket. 'You've got a very good shape for the jive. If he's asleep, poke him in the ribs and wake him up. He won't want to have missed you.'

Hannah made her way past a pond, down some steps and then across the lawn to where Douglas was lying on a rug in front of the summerhouse.

He sat up as soon as he saw her.

'Hi,' said Hannah. 'Did you know that most of your answers in that maths test were wrong?'

'Oh . . . yes,' said Douglas. 'Well, I didn't at the time, but I . . . I'm sorry if I got you into trouble.'

'You did.' Hannah sat down on the rug beside him. 'But it turned out OK. That's what I came to tell you about really. If you're interested.'

Douglas said he certainly was. He was very curious to know what had happened when Hannah's father found her in Norwich.

Hannah put her arms round her legs and rested her

chin on her knees. 'I ran away to where I used to live,' she said, 'but my dad came and found me.'

'I heard,' said Douglas. 'Was he very angry?'

'No, that was the weird thing. He wasn't angry at all.'

Hannah had expected him to be angry. She remembered the shock of hearing her father's voice as he arrived at Laura's house and her determination that she was not going to give up and go home with him, whatever he threatened and however loudly he shouted. But, to her surprise he had not threatened or shouted at all.

He had come striding up the stairs to the attic room, straight over to the wardrobe in which she was hiding, as if he knew exactly where she was, flung open the door and then . . . sat down beside her and asked if they could talk.

They had talked for nearly two hours. Hannah had told him about not wanting to move and how she wanted to be back in Norwich with her friends, and Mr Linneker told her about the stresses of being in a new job and how, even when you loved people, you could still make mistakes.

'Maybe we can negotiate a solution on this one,' he had said in the end. 'If you tell me exactly what you want, I'll tell you what I want, and we'll try and work out some way we both get as much of what we want as we can.'

'And did you?' asked Douglas.

Hannah nodded. 'I've been staying in Norwich over half-term, and I can go back again in the holidays. Dad says he hadn't realized how much I wanted to be there. He says it's good when you know what you want like that. He says it's the people that don't know that have the real problem.'

Douglas nodded but said nothing.

There was a large spider crawling up Hannah's leg and she picked it up and put it back on the grass before saying, 'How did you know?'

'What?'

'Where I'd gone.' She looked directly at Douglas. 'I know it was you, Dad didn't want to tell me but I made him. He thinks I told you where I was going before I ran away, but I didn't. So how did you know?'

'I'd like to tell you sometime,' said Douglas, 'but I can't at the moment.'

Hannah nodded.

'If I shouldn't have done it, I'm sorry,' Douglas went on, 'but at the time it seemed like the best thing to do.'

'I wasn't complaining,' said Hannah. 'I don't know why, but it all turned out rather well.'

After that they talked about what it was like to be hit by lightning, and when Douglas would be coming back to school – he thought the next day – and what it was like to live in Norwich . . . And then Hannah noticed it was gone five o'clock and past the time she was supposed to be home.

Douglas walked her back to the house and as they crossed the hall to the front door, he said, 'If your dad is right, and knowing what you want is a good thing, what happens if you know what you want, but it turns out to be something you can't have?'

They were standing out in the drive, with the sunshine pouring down through the trees sending a pattern of dappled light on to the gravel.

Hannah gave a little shrug. 'I suppose you could scream and shout and make a nuisance of yourself until they say you can have it,' she said. 'It worked for me.'

Douglas thought, rather sadly, that making a nuisance of himself might not have too much effect on a Guardian of the Federation.

'I'll see you tomorrow,' said Hannah but instead of walking away, she turned to Douglas, put her arms round his neck and held him very tightly for a moment. Then she released him as quickly as she had seized him and set off down the driveway without a word.

There was something in the way she walked that reminded him of Kai, Douglas thought. There was that same sense of determination and purpose in her movements, as if she knew exactly where she was going and what she would do when she got there.

At the bottom of the drive she turned.

'Something my dad told me,' she called back. 'He said, before you kick and scream and make a nuisance of yourself, you should try telling people what you want. He said, if you ask, sometimes that's all it takes.'

And with a wave she was gone.

CHAPTER FIFTEEN

Three days later Guardian Quomp came back. Douglas was in his bedroom doing some homework and trying not to remember how much easier it had been when he had Gedrus to give him all the answers, when he heard a tapping at the window.

The Guardian was outside the first-floor window, standing on a small, flat, floating disc.

'You're looking a lot better than the last time I saw you!' he said when Douglas opened the window. 'How are you feeling?'

Douglas thought the Guardian was looking much better himself as he stood there, fingering the green crystal round his neck and beaming happily down.

'I'm fine,' said Douglas. 'Thank you.'

'Good!' The Guardian swayed slightly on the disc, as he thrust his hands in his pockets. 'And how's the heart? You know we gave you a new one? An improvement on the one you had before I might add. If you ever want to take up long-distance running you'll find you have incredible stamina.'

'Yes,' said Douglas. 'Ivo told me.'

'Well, there's a couple of things we ought to talk about and I thought, as your parents are out, that this might be a good time. But if it's not convenient I could call back later.'

'No, that's fine.' Douglas pushed open the window. 'Would you like to come in?'

The Guardian looked at the size of the window and then at the size of his waist. 'Might be safer if I came down to the back door.' He pointed rather proudly to the disc beneath his feet. 'Have you seen this? Got it today. You just lean the way you want to go and whoosh! I'll meet you down there!'

He leaned to the right and flew off at an alarming speed towards the trees at the side of the house.

When Douglas got down to the kitchen the Guardian was already waiting at the back door, carrying the disc under one arm. 'If there was any chance of a cup of tea,' he said, pulling a couple of leaves out of his hair and brushing a moss stain from his elbow, 'it would be more than welcome.'

Douglas made a pot of tea and Quomp breathed in a mug of scalding hot liquid with a sigh of satisfaction.

'Right then, first things first.' He took a box from his pocket and opened it to reveal what looked like a brooch in the shape of a tiny bunch of flowers. 'I've been asked to give you this.'

'What is it?' asked Douglas.

'It's the Flaggiano Cluster.' The Guardian took the flowers carefully from the box. 'It's a Federation award for bravery – well, *the* award, really.'

He stepped forward and pinned the brooch to the front of Douglas's T-shirt.

'On behalf of the Presiding Council of the Order of Guardians, it is my proud privilege to present this to you with the grateful thanks of the Federation for your help in the safe return of four stolen Touchstones.'

'Oh,' said Douglas. 'Thank you very much.'

'It's the only plant able to grow in deep space.' The Guardian pointed to the brooch. 'They can withstand temperatures from absolute zero to 5000 degrees centigrade. If you splash a bit of water on them every couple of centuries, they'll flower for a thousand years.'

'I'll try and remember that,' said Douglas.

'OK, ceremony over.' The Guardian returned to the table to pour himself another cup of tea. 'But I want you to know I meant that bit about the grateful thanks of the Federation. What might have happened if Kai had got away, I dread to think, and the only reason she didn't is you.'

'What happened to her?' asked Douglas. 'Is she dead?'

'No, no, no, no, no!' Quomp frowned. 'I'm happy

to say she's safely locked up and awaiting trial on Molnok, screaming to everyone that her planet has been betrayed and the Federation let her down.' His frown deepened. 'And the worst of it is, she has a point. Her homeworld's in a right mess and how the local Guardian let it get like that is a complete mystery. However, that's no excuse for stealing four Touchstones, or killing you for that matter, even if it was an accident. I really was very cross with her about that.'

'So what's going to happen to her?'

'It's going to take several hundred lawyers to decide that one,' said the Guardian with a sigh. 'Ask me again in a couple of years.'

'And the Touchstone? The one she had?'

'Yes?' Quomp pulled out a chair and sat himself down at the table. 'What about it?'

'I was wondering what you'd done with it.' Douglas hesitated. 'I suppose what I really want to know is what happened to the one I had. In fact, I've been wondering,' he went on, 'if there was any way I could have it back.'

'Oh you have, have you?' Quomp leaned back in his seat and looked at Douglas over the top of his glasses.

'I know you said how dangerous it was to let someone like me have a Touchstone.' Douglas sat himself at the table, facing the Guardian. 'But couldn't there be some way round that? I mean, didn't the Yōb have some sort of child control, like we do on the Internet?

Isn't there some way you could let me have the stone but without letting me make bombs or start plagues? And in return maybe I could do something useful.'

'Like what?' said Quomp.

'Well, I'm not sure, but there must be something. Nobody else can use the Touchstone I had, can they? And it seems a terrible waste for it never to be used again.'

He paused, waiting for the Guardian to answer, but Quomp did not speak. He sat there looking at Douglas, as if waiting for him to say something else.

'What I was hoping,' Douglas went on, 'what I was hoping was that you'd ask Gedrus if he knows of any way I could have my Touchstone back. If he says it's a bad idea and I shouldn't have it then fine, I won't. I mean, I wouldn't want it if Gedrus said it was going to lead to trouble, but if he thought it might be all right, that it might be useful, then I'd really like to have it back.' He paused and added, 'I think it's the only thing in the world I really do want. So could you ask him, please?'

Quomp still did not answer directly. Instead he put his hand in his pocket, took out a Touchstone and held it thoughtfully in the palm of his hand.

'Well . . .' he said eventually, 'if you want it that badly, I suppose we'd better let you have it.' And he reached across the table and carefully placed the stone around Douglas's neck.

Douglas was rather confused. He'd expected a little more resistance than this.

'You might want to check I've given you the right one,' said Quomp.

Douglas reached up and as his fingers met the Touchstone, the familiar figure of Gedrus appeared in the air in front of him. He was sitting at his chair in the library, just as he had that first day, his feet up on the desk in front of him, reading a book and eating an apple.

'Hi there!' He waved cheerily. 'Long time no see. What can I do for you?'

'Nothing really,' said Douglas. 'Well, not at the moment. I just wanted to check you were still there.'

'Always here, old buddy.' Gedrus turned the page of his book and took another bite of his apple. 'Always here. Ready and waiting.'

And in that moment, Douglas felt a great weight slide from his shoulders. He did not quite know what the weight had been or why it had suddenly gone, but he did know that holding the Touchstone in his hand felt *right*.

Quomp was looking at him.

'You're giving it to me? Just like that?'

'That's the plan,' said Quomp.

'Aren't you going to ask Gedrus if it's a good idea?'

The Guardian gave a little smile. 'Oh, I asked him that some time ago! For some reason he seemed to think it would be an excellent idea.'

'But . . .' Douglas hesitated. 'But I thought the rule was that only Guardians are allowed to have a Touchstone? Are you allowed to change it?'

'I have no intention of changing any of the rules,' said Quomp firmly, 'least of all that one. Basis of everything. No, no, the rule stands.'

He smiled again, and it was a moment before Douglas fully realized what he meant. Even when he did, he could hardly believe it.

The Guardian held out his hand.

'Welcome to the Order, Douglas,' he said.

'You're a Guardian?' said Ivo. It was the third time he had asked the question and he was still unable to keep the disbelief out of his voice.

'Sort of a trainee, junior, novice, apprentice Guardian.' Douglas did not find the whole thing easy to believe himself. 'But yes. I'm a Guardian.'

They were sitting in Ivo's new workshop. It was larger than his old shed, with gleaming new work-benches running down one side and an impressive selection of power tools on the other. The two boys were on a battered sofa at one end, where Ivo had his plastered foot propped up on a cushion as he tried to absorb the news.

'So what happens now?' he asked. 'You go off and rule the universe or something?'

'It's not quite like that,' said Douglas. 'As far as I can tell, all Guardians actually *do* is answer questions.

People want to know something, I ask Gedrus for them, and pass on whatever he says.'

'What people?'

'Anyone really,' Douglas shrugged. 'Anyone who's passing.'

Quomp had told him that, out here on the edge of the Federation, passing ships would be limited to the occasional merchant vessel or troop carrier, so he probably wouldn't see more than a dozen or so people a week.

'And what happens if they ask you how to do something bad?' said Ivo. 'Like Kai wanting to steal some Touchstones. What do you tell them then?'

'I say whatever Gedrus tells me to say,' said Douglas. 'I don't actually ask him the question people give me. Guardians never do that. I say to Gedrus, "This person has asked me this question, what's the best thing I can say in reply?"'

'Best for who?' asked Ivo. 'Best for you, best for them . . .'

'Just . . . best,' said Douglas. 'You know, for everyone.'

'And then they go and do whatever you told them?'

'If they do,' said Douglas, 'it seems to work out. Quomp says that's what happens when you ask the right question. It's because Gedrus knows what people really want. He knows what they ought to be doing, where they ought to be going . . . so when they do what he says, it's like they suddenly find they're heading in the right direction and their problems seem to get sorted out.'

'Like your parents,' said Ivo.

Exactly like his parents, Douglas thought. Mr and Mrs Paterson were still separated but that didn't stop them being a lot happier these days. And they were getting on better with each other as well. When his father brought him home after their trip to the cinema on Saturday, he had actually come into the house, stayed for a cup of tea and then fixed the tap in the downstairs lavatory. He had even offered to drive the coach when Mrs Paterson took her party of under fourteens to the qualifying heats of the Jive and Disco Championship in Manchester.

One of the dancers she would be taking was Hannah Linneker, who had recently started jive classes and showed, Mrs Paterson said, all the athleticism and complete lack of fear that you needed to be thrown several metres into the air while relying on your partner to catch you. Mind you, her partner was David Collins and Douglas thought he'd be far too frightened to let her fall. If he did, Hannah might stick his head in a fire bucket again.

'Is there a charge?' asked Ivo. 'When people ask you these questions? Do they have to give you money?'

'No,' said Douglas. 'No, it's all free.'

'In that case,' Ivo said, looking rather relieved, 'can

I ask you something about the driveshaft housing on the robot?'

'Sure,' said Douglas and he watched as Ivo hopped over to the workbench to collect a long tube of metal connected to the electric motor from a washing machine.

As he watched, he wondered why it was that his best friend should turn out to be an accident-prone Bulgarian who ate raw onions for lunch. He had read somewhere that the strongest friendships are often forged in times of crisis and shared danger and it was true that, from the time they had both carried Kai's body down to the bathroom in the annexe, they had had plenty of both.

But it was more than that. There had always been something very reassuring about being with Ivo and only now did Douglas realize why. The fact was that Ivo was the one person he knew who had *always* been on the right compass heading. Ivo had always known where he was going and what he wanted. He had always been just . . . Ivo.

'I think there's a problem with the flange setting.' Ivo was back and holding out the tube of metal. 'I used longer bolts because they were all I had, but I'm wondering if that means there won't be room for the axle connection.'

He waited patiently while Douglas fingered the Touchstone hanging round his neck and asked Gedrus.

'He says it'll be fine.' Douglas released the stone and turned to his friend. 'He says there's nothing to worry about. It's all going to be just fine.'

'You've got five visitors,' Guardian Quomp explained. 'A merchant from Galatea, a Commodore in the Federation Navy, two politicians from Nuuk and the Mimbari amabassador. Are you ready?'

'I think so.' Douglas was standing in the little sitting room of the annexe where Kai had stayed nearly two months before. He was wearing his school clothes, with the Touchstone hanging down neatly over his tie.

'Nervous?' asked Quomp.

'No, not really.'

'Quite right.' Quomp nodded vigorously. 'Absolutely no need. Nothing to worry about at all. I send them in, they ask their question, and . . .'

'. . . and I ask Gedrus what's the best thing I can say in reply.'

'Precisely. That's all there is to it.' The Guardian looked anxiously at Douglas. 'Don't forget to use *exactly* the words Gedrus says. Never mind if they sound odd, or rude or you don't understand them – whatever Gedrus tells you, that's what you say.'

'OK,' said Douglas.

'Attaboy!' Quomp gave him an encouraging pat on the shoulder before heading back to the door. 'The first one's the Galatean – I did warn you they were incredibly ugly, didn't I?'

'Yes, you did,' said Douglas.

'They've got this gunge that dribbles out of their ears when they get excited but don't take any notice.' Quomp paused and took a deep breath. 'Right, well, I'll send him in then.'

The Guardian disappeared. There was a shuffling sound from the corridor and a moment later a short figure with loosely hanging skin, almost entirely covered in warts and tufts of bristly hair, entered the room. A substance like green custard dripped from his ears on to his shoulders and a sharp, pungent smell filled the air.

Douglas did not even notice. At that moment, nothing could disturb the peace and contentment he felt. Like Ivo with his robot, like his mother at a dance class, like his father at the garage building his supermarket trolley, he found he was exactly where he wanted to be, doing exactly what he wanted. He had no idea where it might lead him but that didn't matter. The compass needle was pointing due north and the road ahead was straight and clear.

He raised a hand in greeting to the alien.

'Hi there!' he said. 'What can I do for you?'